For Laura Wininger and Jeffrey Isaac

If not for your hospitality when
we were snowbound in Colorado,
the Sisters Eight would never have
been born. Thank you for a lifetime
of love and friendship.

Annie   Durinda   Georgia   Jackie

Marcia   Petal   Rebecca   Zinnia

PROLOGUE

Are you still here?

Or did you just walk in?

Very well . . .

Once upon a time there were eight sisters who would all one day be eight years old. At the same time. You know: octuplets.

Their names were Annie, Durinda, Georgia, Jackie, Marcia, Petal, Rebecca, and Zinnia. They were each born a minute apart on August 8, 2000. All eight had brown hair and brown eyes. And although they were all the same exact age, give or take a few minutes, each was one inch taller than the next, with Zinnia being the shortest and Annie the tallest.

On New Year's Eve 2007, their parents disappeared, or died. Their mother went into the kitchen for eggnog, their father went out to the woodshed for firewood, and neither returned.

Now the Eights must figure out what happened to

their parents while keeping the outside world from discovering that eight little girls are home alone.

At the beginning of their first adventure, also known as *The Sisters Eight, Book 1: Annie's Adventures,* the girls became aware of the disappearance of their parents, and they found a note hidden behind a loose stone in the wall of the drawing room of their magnificent home. The note read:

Dear Annie, Durinda, Georgia, Jackie, Marcia, Petal, Rebecca, and Zinnia,

This may come as rather a shock to you, but it appears you each possess a power and a gift. The powers you already have—you merely don't know you have them yet. The gifts are from your parents, and these you must also discover for yourselves. In fact, you must each discover both your power and your gift in order to reveal what happened to your parents. Have you got all that?

The note was unsigned.

During the course of *Book 1: Annie's Adventures,* Annie discovered her power: the ability to be as smart as an adult when needed. She also discovered her gift: a lovely ring with a purple gemstone in it.

Then, in *Book 2: Durinda's Dangers,* Durinda discovered *her* power: by tapping her leg three times rapidly and then pointing at a person, she could make that person freeze. Except Zinnia, of course. No matter what anyone did, no one could make Zinnia freeze. And Durinda also discovered *her* gift: beautiful earrings the color of emeralds.

By the end of the second book, the Eights, as they are known, realized there was a pattern to the madness: each month one of them, starting with the oldest and working down, would discover her own power and gift. Annie discovered hers in January, and Durinda discovered hers in February. This meant that in March, it would be Georgia's turn.

Oh, dear.

Oh, deary dear.

And one final *oh, dear:* Have you noticed something odd? Is a book *talking* to you? Well, I suppose it's better than your *refrigerator* doing the talking . . .

And what *did* happen to the Eights' parents? Well, we don't know that yet, do we? Besides, if I told you that now, I would be *telling* and not *showing* . . .

CHAPTER ONE

"It was a dark and stormy night," Rebecca said.

It was that. It was also the first of March, a Saturday.

"I believe that line has been used before," Jackie pointed out to Rebecca.

Jackie read more books than any of us. Some of us thought she read *too* much. But whenever any of us tried to mention that, she told us that such a thing was impossible.

We were all in the front room, looking out the window, watching the rain pour down. Daddy Sparky, the suit of armor we dressed up so nosy people peeking in would think our real daddy was there, sat in his usual chair, the big comfy one. Mommy Sally, the dressmaker's dummy we dressed up to look like our real mommy, was standing at his side, wearing a sleeveless purple dress and a string of pearls. Daddy Sparky and Mommy Sally weren't much good at conversation, but at least they provided *some* adult company. Plus, they were both smart dressers.

"It was raining cats and dogs," Annie said, thinking to improve on Rebecca's opening line. That was Annie all over: always trying to one-up the rest of us.

"I think that would be very scary for the cats," Petal said. "In fact, I know Precious wouldn't want to be part of a downpour."

We had eight gray-and-white puffballs that were our cats, one for each sister. Their names were Anthrax, Dandruff, Greatorex, Jaguar, Minx, Precious, Rambunctious, and Zither. Precious was Petal's cat.

Well, we sighed, at least Petal was worrying about someone other than herself for a change, even if that someone was a cat.

"March is coming in like a lion," Durinda began.

"But are you completely sure it will go out like a lamb?" Zinnia asked.

"If this were April," Marcia observed, "we could have showers that would bring May flowers."

"Would you all just *stop?*" Georgia shouted.

"Did we say something wrong?" Jackie asked.

Georgia continued to stare out into the dark and stormy night as the rain machine-gunned our windows.

"Why does *my* month have to be riddled with clichés?" Georgia finally whined.

"What's a cliché?" Petal wanted to know.

Not only did Petal worry more than any person who ever lived, she also didn't pay attention during vocabulary lessons at the Whistle Stop, the school where we were all third-graders. We tried to tell her that vocabulary was important, but she always told *us* that to *her* it was all just so many words, words, words.

"A cliché," Annie said, as though she were reciting from a dictionary, "is a trite phrase or expression. Also, a hackneyed theme, characterization, or situation."

"Great." Rebecca sneered. "And what do *trite* and *hackneyed* mean? Don't even bother defining *characterization*. I'm sure it doesn't concern us."

"Trite," Annie said, "is when something becomes hackneyed or boring from too much use. It means not fresh, not original. *Hackneyed* means lacking in freshness or originality. Also, it means trite."

"Trite is hackneyed, hackneyed is trite." Rebecca rolled her eyes. "Well, *that* clears it all up. Why can't the people who write dictionaries just agree on one word for it?"

"Exactly," Georgia said. "And that one word should be *cliché*." She sulked some more, pressing her nose against the glass. "I don't know why *my* month has to be riddled with—"

C-RASH!

S-LAM!

THUMP!

Yes, that was when the carrier pigeon struck the other side of the windowpane that Georgia's nose was pressed against. The carrier pigeon's little body struck the glass with more force than . . . well, than any carrier pigeon's body had ever thumped against glass before.

We were used to carrier pigeons visiting the house and bringing notes. They were Daddy's friends. And even now that he was gone, wherever he'd gone to, they still came. But they'd never before come in the midst of a dark and stormy night.

"Well, let it in. Let it in!" Durinda cried, pushing Georgia out of the way and opening the window for the pigeon.

The pigeon, looking about as grateful as we'd ever seen a pigeon look, hopped onto Durinda's outstretched finger.

"Poor little pigeon," Durinda cooed. "All your feathers are soaked."

Just as Annie performed a lot of the daddy functions around the household in the absence of our real daddy, Durinda had turned out to be the most motherly. And we had grown used to things being that way. Really, Daddy Sparky and Mommy Sally might have been sharp dressers, but there was nothing like having real human beings to tuck you in at night, to show you love when you needed it.

"There, there." Durinda continued to soothe the pigeon,

using her other hand to stroke its sopping feathers. Then a puzzled look came over Durinda's face. "Hey," she said, "what's this strapped under your wing?"

"It's probably just another one of those stupid notes," Georgia grumped.

"No, I don't think so," Marcia said. "The notes always come rolled up inside the little metal tube attached to the pigeon's leg. And this pigeon *has* one of those tubes on his leg, so that can't be it."

After much fumbling, Durinda's searching fingers produced a waterproof sack that was cinched with a drawstring. The drawstring was not waterproof, so it was dripping.

"Here." Durinda handed it to Georgia. "You open it. I can't take care of the pigeon, hold the sack, and open it and remove whatever is in it all at the same time."

"She's right," Petal said. "I'm pretty sure she would need at least one extra hand to do all of that."

So, still grumping, Georgia took the sack.

"I don't know why I always have to do all the work around here," she grumbled.

We all glared at her. Georgia hardly ever did *any* work, unless it was mischief.

"The drawstring on this sack is dripping all over my socks," Georgia complained.

"Just open it!" Zinnia hurried her along. "I think it must be one of our gifts!"

"Why in the world would you think a stupid thing like . . . Hello!" Georgia said, wonder filling her face as she removed a gold object from the sack. The object looked like a compact case, and on the front of it was engraved the name *Georgia*.

"What's this?" Georgia asked.

"It's your gift, obviously." Now it was Zinnia's turn to sulk. "I was kind of hoping that the order had been switched around, that somehow it would turn out to be *my* gift."

Jackie put her arm around Zinnia and gave her shoulders a squeeze. Whenever Annie or Durinda didn't take care of us right away, Jackie was good at filling the gap.

"Fine," Georgia said. "So it's my gift." She kept turning it around in her fingers, held it up to the light, squinted at it. "But *what* is it?"

"Haven't you ever seen a compact before?" Rebecca asked. "I'll bet anything there's a mirror inside there."

She made a kissy face with her lips. "You're supposed to look in the mirror to check your lipstick and make sure you look bea-*u*-ti-ful."

"But I don't wear lipstick!" Georgia was clearly annoyed. "Do I *look* like the kind of girl who would have any need for a compact mirror?"

We studied Georgia closely, and we had to admit: she didn't. Really, had she even bothered to comb her hair today?

"I have to say, Georgia," Annie said, "you're probably the only person in the history of the world who has ever looked a gift horse in the mouth."

"It's a gift compact," Georgia said, "and stop talking in clichés. It's trite." She paused and considered. "I'm pretty sure it's hackneyed too." She sighed a heavy sigh. "Just my luck," she said. "I get my gift, and it's not even anything I would ever want. What's next? Will my power be something useless too?"

"I should think you'd be more grateful," Zinnia said with an unusual show of spirit. "At least you got your gift. While some of us are still waiting—"

"Hey! Wait a second!" Annie snapped her fingers. "No matter that you don't like your gift, Georgia—each power and gift we find brings us one step closer to discovering what happened to Mommy and Daddy!"

"But isn't it a bit odd," Jackie said, "Georgia finding her gift at the *beginning* of the month, instead of at the end of it, like what usually happens? Plus, she didn't exactly find it. You could say that *it* found *her*." Jackie really was puzzled, a rare thing. "It just doesn't make any sense for the gift to arrive now, and like this."

"We never did read the note the pigeon brought," Marcia pointed out.

"Read it!" Petal cried.

"Read it!" Zinnia cried.

So Durinda, still carefully handling the wet pigeon, removed the tiny metal tube from its leg and took out the scroll of paper from the tube.

"Look at Durinda go now," Rebecca said. "It's like she suddenly has three hands."

Durinda ignored Rebecca, which was a habit among us. First, Durinda read whatever was written on the scroll to herself, her lips working while she did.

"Do you think you could read it aloud," Annie asked, "so we can all hear it?"

"It says," Durinda said, "'We're delivering her gift early, because we just can't bear to hear Georgia whine all month.'"

Then Durinda looked down at the pigeon in her hand.

"How," Durinda said, addressing the pigeon, "did you ever fly all the way here from wherever you came from with that sack holding the compact folded under your wing? It can't have been easy flying like that."

The pigeon gazed straight back at Durinda. We couldn't be certain, but it looked as though the pigeon shrugged.

"What kind of note is that?" Georgia demanded. Her face was practically purple with rage. "This is supposed to be *my* month, and yet even the note insults me!"

"But at least you got your gift," Zinnia said, "and you got it early, at that. I wonder, if I were to whine like you do all the time, could I make my gift come early?"

"But this is still all wrong," Jackie said. "The return with the elixir isn't supposed to happen until near the end of the story."

"The return with the *what?*" Rebecca looked peeved. "What are you talking about, Jackie?"

"The return with the *elixir*," Jackie repeated patiently.

"There are a lot of involved definitions of *elixir*," Annie said, "but it's basically just a wonderful thing."

"I've been reading a book on screenwriting," Jackie went on, as if Annie hadn't spoken. This was odd; we did that to Rebecca, Georgia too, but never to Annie.

"What's screenwriting?" Petal asked.

"It's writing scripts for movies and things," Annie said. She was clearly miffed at Jackie's snub. "You do all know what movies are, don't you?"

"Anyway," Jackie continued, "the book says that only

after the heroine or heroines have gone through their entire adventure, only then does she or they return with the elixir. It's like coming home with a prize. It's the last of twelve stages."

"Then I really don't want this now!" Georgia cried. She took the compact with her name engraved on it and forced it back up under the pigeon's wing.

The pigeon looked startled, as did we all.

"Take it back, you bloody pigeon!" Georgia cried. "I don't want it now if it's not the proper time." Georgia hustled the poor little pigeon out the window—really, we thought, the poor little thing was only doing his job. Georgia yelled after him as he flew away, "And don't come back until the end of the month!" then slammed the window shut.

There, we thought, Georgia had handled *that* well.

A moment of stunned silence followed, then we heard Rebecca tsk-tsk into the void.

"What are you tsk-tsking about now?" Georgia demanded.

"It's just, you know." Rebecca shrugged. "Only you, Georgia."

"What's that supposed to mean?" The beginning of *her* month having been riddled with clichés, Georgia was obviously in no mood for riddles. "Only me, what?"

"She means," Annie said, "that only you would send your gift back to wherever our gifts come from."

"Huh." The anger had disappeared from Georgia's face like a pigeon flying off into the night. She was puzzled. "You mean I wasn't supposed to do that?"

We didn't like to be insulting, but . . .

"Duh!" we all shouted at her.

Once we had stopped shouting, and Georgia had gotten over being shouted at, Marcia spoke.

"You know," she said, "usually whenever one of us discovers her power or gift, there's a new note left in the space behind that loose stone in the wall of the drawing room."

With that in mind, we all trooped off to the drawing room.

"You do the honors," Annie said to Georgia as we stood before the wall. "It was your gift."

"Yeah," Rebecca said, "until she gave it back."

Ignoring Rebecca, Georgia carefully removed the loose

stone. Then she reached into the space and pulled out a note. We all crowded around her to read what it said:

Dear Georgia,

This is the part where I'd normally say, "Nice work. Five down, eleven to go." But, sadly, I can't do that this time, can I?

As always, the note was unsigned.

Georgia looked so sad that we couldn't help feeling sorry for her, despite what she'd done.

We watched as Georgia let go of the note; it floated idly down to the floor like a feather on a breeze.

"It's still only the first day of my month," she said glumly, "and already I'm not handling things very well, am I."

We tried to *there, there* her—not just Annie and Durinda and even Jackie, but all of us. But that dark and stormy night, there were not enough *there, there*s in the world to soothe Georgia's upset feelings.

If only Daddy Sparky and Mommy Sally were our real mommy and daddy, we thought as we put Georgia to bed. They could have at least helped us kiss her good night before we turned out the lights.

CHAPTER TWO

The next day, Sunday, passed in silence and misery.

This was all Georgia's fault, of course. She was so sad that she'd blown her big chance to receive her gift early that she spent the whole day moping around the house in her bathrobe and slippers.
It didn't help any of our
moods that it was still
raining so hard.
This meant that
we couldn't even
go outside to play,
which at least would
have gotten us away from
Georgia's endless whining.

"Perhaps a nice cup of tea would cheer you up," Durinda offered Georgia. "Shall I make you a cup of tea? Or coffee?"

"I don't drink tea," Georgia groused from her curled-up position on the sofa. She had placed a hot-water bottle on her head.

"Are you an invalid?" Rebecca asked her, pointing at the hot-water bottle. "Maybe you will die a gruesome death and then we will all have to mourn you." She shrugged. "At least that would leave more frosting for me."

We all knew how much frosting meant to Rebecca.

"None of us drink tea," Georgia said to Durinda, ignoring Rebecca. "Can't you remember that? And only Annie ever drinks coffee."

"The rest of us like juice," Jackie said.

"Mango, if we can get it," Zinnia added.

"I do believe Georgia is starting to look genuinely sick," Marcia observed.

"That may be," Annie said, "but it's no reason for her to snap at Durinda so. She was only trying to help. Besides, if Georgia's not careful, Durinda might get angry and then tap her leg three times, point at Georgia, and make her freeze."

"Do you think we could get Durinda to do that even if she's not angry?" Rebecca asked hopefully.

"This rain worries me," Petal said, looking out the window.

"Why?" Annie asked. "At least it's made the last of the snow wash away."

"Yes," Petal said. "But it just keeps going on and on. It's not natural! Do you think it will rain for forty days and forty nights, and we will have to build an ark to sail away in before we all drown?"

"No," Rebecca said firmly. Then she got a teasing gleam in her eye. "It might rain for thirty-nine days and thirty-nine nights, but it will surely stop before it gets to forty."

"Do you really think it'll rain for thirty-nine days and thirty-nine nights?" Petal asked.

If someone didn't say something sensible, Petal would work herself into such a worrying frenzy, she'd spin right up into outer space.

"No," Annie said. "Rebecca is just pulling your leg."

"But why would she want to do that?" Petal said. "If she keeps pulling my leg, and it's always the same leg, one leg will eventually be longer than the other. Then I will be lopsided and people will make fun of me wherever I go. They will all say, 'Ooh, look! Here comes Lopsided Petal!'" She shuddered. "It will be awful."

Annie threw up her hands. "I give up," she said. "Why don't you put on your bouncy boots and go bounce in the drawing room for a while."

Bouncy boots, one of Mommy's inventions, were the puffy silver boots that had been our biggest present the year before. When we wore them on our feet, they made us bounce high with each step we took. But we could use them only in the drawing room, with its high cathedral ceiling, because Mommy had accidentally put too much bounce in them. When we tried to use them in any of the other rooms, we bounced too high and our heads hit the ceiling.

But Petal was in no mood for bouncing just then.

"I can't believe I just let my gift fly out the window!" Georgia moaned from her position on the sofa. Then she sighed a great sigh. "Am I really the stupidest Eight who ever lived?"

"No, you're not," said Jackie. "After all, we might have some relatives somewhere that we don't know about yet."

"You could be," Marcia said. "But first, we'd need to do a scientific survey to find out."

"I don't think it's worth worrying about," Annie said. "Robot Betty is dumber than you are, if it makes you feel any better, but that's probably not what you had in mind."

Robot Betty, another one of Mommy's inventions, was supposed to clean our house, but she hardly ever got anything right.

"Would you like me to make you some cocoa?" Durinda offered. "Oh, and Carl the talking refrigerator is dumber than you are too, at least when he's in love.

But Carl's not a blood relative, and neither is robot Betty, so I don't think either one of them counts."

"If you were the stupidest Eight who ever lived," Petal fretted, "this could be very bad for the rest of us. I mean, what if one day you do something even more stupid than this, and then we all *die?*" She paused for a moment's thought, then addressed the room at large. "The cats are all definitely smarter than Georgia, and the cats *are* family. But what about the plants? Do plants count?"

"If I tell you that you're not the stupidest Eight," Zinnia offered Georgia, "will you buy me a gift?"

"Yes, you are the stupidest Eight," Rebecca said. "Now get over it."

So that was what our day was like—soggy and moany—and our night was no better.

It didn't even get better when Jackie, hoping to snap Georgia out of her funk, suggested we do our Waltons routine at bedtime.

The Waltons is this show that was on television sometime in the last century. Mommy once brought a DVD of it home for us to watch. She said something about how maybe if we watched it, we'd be more interested in doing chores around the house, since all of the Walton kids had to do chores and they always looked so happy to be doing them.

But the Waltons lived on a farm. We, however, didn't, and we had no cows to milk or hens to collect eggs from, and although we would have liked to have had a small horse to exercise, we didn't have one of those either. So we'd told Mommy that we didn't think the show applied to us.

As for the tractor on the show, we didn't have one, and if we had had one, we wouldn't have known how to fix it. Still, we did have our own personal mechanic—Pete—whom we'd inherited from Daddy and who was great for helping us out whenever we had any problems with our purple Hummer, which our scientist mother had fixed so it was environment-friendly. Plus, Pete was good at all sorts of other stuff.

We did like watching *The Waltons.* You know: nostalgia. It was about this small family—only seven kids!—although their grandparents lived with them, so we supposed that what with the old people and all the animals, their household was more crowded than ours.

At any rate, at the end of each episode, they'd show the outside of the Walton house with just one light on. The audience couldn't see any of the characters but they could hear the family members call out random good nights to one another from their rooms. We always thought it was a great way to end the day, but sometimes we forgot to do it.

That Sunday night, in a group effort to cheer up Georgia, we remembered.

"Good night, Durinda!" Annie called.

Annie slept in one room with Georgia, Jackie, and Marcia, and Durinda slept in the other with Petal, Rebecca, and Zinnia. It hadn't always been that way. Used to be, the four oldest slept together in one room and the four youngest in another. But when Mommy and Daddy disappeared on New Year's Eve—or died, as Rebecca would have us add—Annie thought it best to make the second-oldest, Durinda, sleep in the room with the youngest three to give them greater comfort. We suspected that none of this sat well with Marcia, who used to be the oldest in the younger bedroom but was now the youngest in the older bedroom. So far, though, Marcia had kept her feelings on this subject to herself.

"Good night, Annie!" Durinda called back. "Good night, Jackie!"

"Good night, Durinda!" Jackie called. "Good night, Petal!"

"Good night, Jackie!" Petal called. "Good night, Rebecca!"

"What are you saying good night to me so loudly for?" Rebecca wanted to know. "I'm right here in the same room with you, Petal." Then: "Good night, Marcia!"

"Good night, Rebecca!" Marcia called. "Good night, Zinnia!"

"Good night, Marcia!" Zinnia called. "Good night, Rebecca!"

"Would you two stop doing that?" Rebecca groused. "Can't you remember I'm in here too?"

"Good night, Georgia!" seven Eights called at the exact same moment.

But even the old reliable Waltons routine didn't help any.

"Good night," Georgia said softly as Annie switched off the last light and the house went dark.

* * * * * * * *

Just as Sunday always follows Saturday, so Monday must follow Sunday . . . unless something happens to stop Monday from coming.

But nothing happened to cancel Monday that week. This meant that the morning after Georgia had gone so quietly to sleep, even *she* had to get ready for school.

"But I'm still so depressed!" Georgia complained when Annie ripped the sheets off her.

"I don't care," Annie said. "Education is important, so you're going. We're *all* going."

So we all put on our wretched yellow plaid uniforms and went.

"Do you think this bus is one of those amphibious vehicles?" Petal asked, her little pink umbrella bobbing over her head as we boarded the bus we now took to the Whistle Stop every school day. "You know, one of those cars that turns into a boat when it becomes surrounded by too much water, like a lake or an ocean?"

"No," Rebecca said.

There were days when we imagined *no* was Rebecca's favorite word in her vocabulary. Even the times she said *yes,* it somehow sounded like *no* to us.

Still, we made it to school without anyone drowning, which we all agreed was a very fine thing.

But when we arrived at our classroom, a trail of wet footprints and tiny puddles behind us, we discovered . . .

"Where's the McG?" Jackie asked.

The McG, whose full name was Mrs. McGillicuddy, was our teacher. She was tall and blond and had an amazingly long nose, which held up her horn-rimmed glasses. She always got to the classroom before we did. We suspected this was to make sure that none of us had the chance to sneak a toad into her desk drawer again.

But on that Monday, that fateful Monday, there was no McG. The only people in the room were our classmates, Mandy Stenko and Will Simms.

Mandy and Will were seated at their desks, hands neatly folded, as though to show they were behaving even though there was no McG in sight.

We liked Will. We liked Will *a lot*. We liked Will so much, we'd even told him the entire story of our parents' disappearance and how we were all now living home alone. As for Mandy, well, we'd been *trying* lately to like her better, particularly since Will had explained to us that Mandy was just jealous of us Eights because we all had one another and she didn't have anyone. But she didn't always make it easy. For example, right now.

"Why don't you put your things away neatly," Mandy suggested, "and wait with us for our teacher to arrive."

"But there's no teacher here *now*," Rebecca countered, tossing her ladybug-pattern raincoat at a coat hook and missing wildly. "So *I* say we have a little *fun*."

For the first time since Saturday, Georgia's expression brightened. "Yes, let's *do*," she said. Then she tossed her own frog-pattern raincoat at a coat hook, also missing wildly.

Before long, there was a pile of eight wildlife-pattern raincoats all over the floor.

Getting into the spirit of things, Will, who had neatly hung up his own yellow slicker before we'd arrived, removed his coat from the hook and added it to our pile.

"What do we do next?" he asked enthusiastically.

This was one of the reasons we liked—no, *loved*— Will: he was always game to get involved with anything we came up with.

"Food fight?" Zinnia suggested shyly. "I've always wanted to take part in one of those."

"No," Annie said sensibly. "We might get hungry for our snacks later, and it will be difficult to eat them if the food is all smooshed."

"Plus, it's wasteful," Durinda added, "and not very nice. You know: people starving in China and all of that."

"I know!" Georgia said, a true gleam in her eye now. "Let's have—drumroll, please—*a spitball fight!*"

"I don't think that's very sanitary," Mandy pointed out, "and it's certainly not ladylike . . ."

But none of us was listening.

We were too busy tearing blank sheets of paper from our notebooks and wadding them up into tiny balls held together by spit and a prayer. We were too busy climbing on chairs and desks—even the McG's desk—so we could take better aim at one another.

We had become, in a word, *mayhem*.

So that's what we were doing—being mayhem—

when the doorknob to the third-grade classroom at the Whistle Stop slowly turned, and in walked Principal Freud accompanied by one of the most gorgeous creatures we'd ever seen.

Principal Freud was bald as an egg, but that didn't matter then. Because we were too busy looking at the creature.

There was something familiar about her. She was probably about ten years younger than our own mommy, and she was tall, like Mommy, and beautiful, like Mommy. She had long hair the color of chestnuts and eyes the color of chocolate, which is nearly everyone's favorite flavor if they're not allergic. Her lips were painted red as a candy apple. And that dress! It had a miniskirt and was mostly turquoise but with swirly patterns in bright pinks and purples and yellows, and just a few dashes of white and black. Really! In addition to being a scientist, our mommy was a great seamstress, but we doubted that even she could make a dress as beautiful as that. And when the woman smiled? It was as if she had thirty-two perfect pearls that had been plucked right from their shells in her mouth. Honestly, she was so beautiful, if there had been an actual halo suspended over her head, it wouldn't have seemed like too much.

So it was really too bad that just as the woman

walked in the door, Georgia, who'd been squatting on the McG's desk waiting to assault Rebecca, let loose with her biggest spitball of all, nailing the beautiful creature smack in the middle of her pretty forehead.

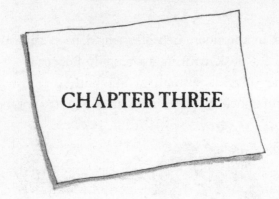

CHAPTER THREE

We had never had a teacher crush before, but we had certainly heard of them. Teacher crushes are when you have a teacher, male or female, who is so wonderful in every way that all the students instantly fall in love with him or her.

There was a good reason we'd never had a teacher crush before. Our kindergarten teacher, Mr. Thimble, whom we'd had for only about five minutes before we were bumped up to first grade, had had long hairs growing out of his nose. People can't help how they look, but these were very distracting nose hairs, and they made it difficult for us to focus on more important things, like finger painting. And our teachers didn't get any better after that, right up through the McG. There was no way a student would ever fall in love with the McG, not unless that student had been tapped by the Crazy Wand.

But this new creature standing next to Principal

Freud, the one Georgia had just beaned in the forehead with the biggest spitball ever?

"This is Serena Harkness." Principal Freud presented the creature to our class.

Even her name was beautiful. It glittered. It was as if the forces of the universe had all gathered together and agreed that no way would she be saddled with an unsuitable name such as Theodora Gumbo.

Before we could try to respond, Principal Freud turned to the creature. This was good, since we were all too awestruck to respond right away.

"Are you sure you're up to this, Ms. Harkness?" he asked gently. "You know, the Eights in particular do have a reputation for being . . . um . . . a little *rough* on teachers. If you'd like, there's still time. We can call in someone else to—"

"Oh, no." Ms. Harkness cut him off with a smile that could have ended wars. "I welcome the challenge."

"Very well," Principal Freud said.

Mandy Stenko raised her hand sharply, as though if someone didn't call on her soon, there might be a bad accident.

"Yes, Mandy?" Principal Freud said.

"Is she a substitute?" Mandy asked.

If we'd been standing closer to Mandy at the time, we would have kicked her. What a question to ask! It was like having guests arrive at your home and asking just a minute after they got there, "So, when are you leaving?" Mommy had told us it was rude every time we'd done it, which was whenever Aunt Martha and Uncle George, our only two relatives outside of our grandparents, had come to stay.

"Ms. Harkness," Principal Freud said with obvious pleasure, "is a little bit, um, *more* than just a regular substitute."

More than a substitute? What did *that* mean? we wondered. Whatever it meant, it sounded very good to us.

Mandy's hand shot straight back up again.

Really, was there ever a girl who needed kicking more than Mandy Stenko?

"Yes, Mandy?" Principal Freud said.

"But what about Mrs. McGillicuddy?" Mandy asked. "Won't she be coming back tomorrow?"

"I'm afraid not," Principal Freud said. "Mrs. McGillicuddy is sick. And, I'm sorry to add, the friend who called on her behalf said that Mrs. McGillicuddy is the kind of sick that will keep her out of school for more than a day. It could be as much as a week. It could be even longer."

Later, when we had a chance to talk among ourselves, we wondered if *we* were the real cause of the McG's extended absence. Had we finally driven her around the bend, as she'd always feared we might?

But there was no time to wonder about that right

then. We had bigger things to think about. For instance, Principal Freud had said that a friend had called the McG in sick. The McG had friends?

Before Mandy could ask any more questions, Principal Freud took one of Ms. Harkness's hands in both of his.

"Then I'll leave you to it, Serena," he said warmly.

"Thank you, Frank," she said back, equally warmly. "I'll be just fine here."

Frank? Now here was a new fact. Principal Freud's first name was *Frank?* When he took off his principal costume and went home at night, he was known around his neighborhood as *Frank Freud?*

Who knew?

Ms. Harkness glided to the center of the room as Principal Freud left, closing the door behind him. Then she looked pointedly—not unpleasantly, as the McG might have done, but definitely pointedly—at the heap of our wet raincoats on the floor. Except for Mandy, whose coat wasn't there in the first place, all of us hurried over to the spot and quietly and neatly put our things where they belonged. This was hardest for Georgia to do, since she had to climb down off the teacher's desk first.

The way that Ms. Harkness had gotten us to put away our things with just a glance—it was like having Mary Poppins in the room, only no one was flying around under an umbrella.

Then, without even being asked to do so—or yelled at to do so, as the McG would have done—we all took our seats in an orderly fashion and folded our hands neatly upon our desks.

Well, all except *one* hand, that is.

Mandy's trigger-happy hand shot straight up into the air again.

"Yes, Mandy?" Ms. Harkness called on her sweetly.

Do you see what we mean about Mandy? They hadn't even been properly introduced yet, and already Ms. Harkness knew her first name. She knew none of ours, but she knew Mandy's.

Okay, we admit it: we were jealous.

"What will we be doing first?" Mandy asked. "Mrs. McGillicuddy always starts with morning meeting." Mandy turned to look at the clock on the wall at the back of the room. "But it's a little late for that now. After morning meeting, we always start with math, unless it's Tuesday, in which case we start with science. But it's Monday, not Tuesday, so perhaps we should start with math right away?"

We wanted to strangle her.

"I'm sure it will come in handy for me," Ms. Harkness said, "you being so familiar with how poor Mrs. McGillicuddy runs her classroom. You'll be able to help me figure out how to do things. But since this is *my* classroom, at least for now, I propose we start off today by doing something a little different."

Different? Did she say *different?* We liked different.

Before Mandy could *yet again* raise the hand that had launched a thousand migraines, Ms. Harkness told us her proposal.

"Principal Freud has already told me a little bit about each of you, the Eights in particular," she said. She even smiled as she said that last part. It was as though she didn't mind at all whatever she'd heard about us!

"But," she went on, "I'd really like to hear you introduce each other in your own words. So we'll start with Mandy and then work our way counterclockwise around the room. Now, then: each of you tell me something vital I should know about the classmate sitting next to you."

Mandy looked stunned at this. It wasn't the sort of assignment she was used to. So she looked at Will, just barely managing to stammer out, "W-will Simms is the only boy in the third grade at the Whistle Stop."

"Thank you, Mandy," Ms. Harkness said. "I'm so glad you pointed that out to me. Will?"

"Annie Huit," Will said with real admiration, "is so smart, sometimes it seems like she doesn't even need a teacher."

"Durinda Huit," Annie said, "cooks pancakes better than nearly anyone in the world."

Durinda sat up a little straighter, hearing that. She hadn't realized her cooking was quite so popular.

"Georgia Huit," Durinda said, "has been awfully depressed lately."

Ms. Harkness floated toward us from her position at the front of the room. She floated until she was standing right in front of Georgia's desk.

"I'm so sorry to hear that," she said, "but you won't be for very long. I'll be keeping a special eye on *you*." Then she bent at the waist, reached out one slender finger, at the end of which was a beautiful long nail painted cotton-candy pink, and tapped Georgia on the nose.

Later, Georgia told us that when Ms. Harkness touched her nose, it felt as though she'd been brushed by magic. We believed her, since when it happened we could swear we saw glittery sparks.

It took Georgia almost a full minute to recover from that touch. When she did, all she could come up with was "Jackie Huit reads too much."

"Marcia Huit," Jackie said, "is very good at observing things. Really, not much that the eye can see gets past her."

"Petal Huit," said Marcia, "worries about everything too much, but we are all trying our best to address that issue."

"I'm worried," Petal said, "that if I don't say the right thing about Rebecca Huit, she will hit me later."

"Oh, I'm sure your sister would never do that," Ms. Harkness said.

For the first time, we saw a flaw in Ms. Harkness's perfection. How could she not see that that was exactly the sort of thing Rebecca would do?

Still, her soothing words had the effect of calming Petal.

"Fine," Petal said. "Pink frosting is never safe around Rebecca Huit."

"Zinnia Huit," Rebecca said, "thinks our cats talk to her."

We all glared at Rebecca, horrified that she'd let the cat out of the bag, so to speak. It was fine for us to make fun of Zinnia when we were all home alone, but it wasn't proper to do so in public. We knew how sensitive Zinnia was about her cat-talking illusions. Or, at any rate, we didn't want strangers to think we were harboring a loony tunes in our family.

"That must be wonderful," Ms. Harkness said to Zinnia. "I've always thought that cats must have so very many more interesting things to talk about than, say, dogs."

Made bold by Ms. Harkness's words, Zinnia opened her mouth to take her turn. But all that came out was "Mandy Stenko has red hair." She paused, then added, "And she raises her hand fairly frequently."

That was our Zinnia all over: always so careful not to say anything that might hurt someone else's feelings.

"Thank you," Ms. Harkness said with a slight bow of her head. "I'm sure the information you've all given me about each other will prove most helpful. Now, then."

Mandy's hand shot up.

"Yes, Mandy?" Ms. Harkness asked.

"Now that we've all introduced one another," Mandy said, "should we start math?" She looked back at the clock again. "Or I suppose maybe English, since that always comes after math and the time for math has passed?"

"No," Ms. Harkness said simply.

"But the time for math *has* passed," Mandy insisted.

"That may be," Ms. Harkness said. "But what would be the fun of doing things the way you always do them on our first day together?"

Fun? First she wanted to do things *different* and now she wanted to have *fun?*

It was like finding ourselves smack in the middle of *Charlie and the Chocolate Factory,* only no one was getting hurt!

"But the *schedule,*" Mandy persisted, pointing to the schedule that the McG always kept taped to the upper-right-hand corner of the blackboard, the blackboard that was really green.

That's when Ms. Harkness turned on her heel—we saw now that she wore high heels, very high; they were leopard-print but somehow managed not to clash with her turquoise dress—and she strode slowly to the blackboard.

We noted that she had a nice stride, like a model's. We knew a lot about how models walked, since our father was one.

Once at the blackboard, Ms. Harkness reached up and peeled off the schedule the McG had taped up there back in September. All that was left on the board were four diagonal marks where the pieces of tape had been. Then Ms. Harkness wadded up the schedule into a ball of paper only slightly bigger than Georgia's infamous spitball and tossed it high in the air. It hung against the fluorescent lights for a full second, like the greatest basketball shot of all time, then dunked into the McG's empty wastebasket.

When the schedule disappeared from view, we did worry, briefly, that Mandy Stenko might faint away and then die. Not that that would have necessarily been such a bad turn of events, but it would have disturbed all the fun we were having. Still, briefly worrying about Mandy did not stop us from shouting, *"Swish!"* right along with Will, and the nine of us pumped our fists in the air.

Ms. Harkness brushed off her hands, one against the other. "There," she said. "Now that that's taken care of, who here is up for recess?"

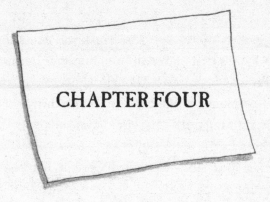

CHAPTER FOUR

"Recess?" Mandy echoed. "But we never have recess until after lunch! And we haven't done any work yet!"

"Besides," Marcia observed—she hated to point it out, but it was the plain truth—"it's raining too hard outside for recess."

"So you'll have it indoors today," Ms. Harkness said brightly.

We sighed. We knew all about indoor recess. It meant staying in the same classroom where we spent the rest of our school day—this room—trying to convince ourselves it was *fun* and *different,* when really the markers and everything else we used were the same things we used during regular classes.

We were so disappointed, we put our elbows onto our desks and sunk our heads down into our open palms.

It was then, in that dark moment, that we heard the most musical of all voices say, "Ready?"

We looked up to see Ms. Harkness standing there holding Petal's little pink umbrella up over her head. The umbrella was open, even though we were . . . *inside!*

This woman was *insane!* The next thing you knew, she'd be running with scissors . . . and she was supposed to be the adult!

In that moment, we loved Serena Harkness even more.

"I think we can all run between the drops to the gymnasium, can't we?" Ms. Harkness suggested.

So that's what we did, running between the drops

behind our new teacher, zigzagging all over the Whistle Stop campus toward the door of the gymnasium. As we ran, Ms. Harkness sang a song, some crazy song involving kittens and whiskers and schnitzel with noodles. The song may have been crazy, but it was enough to distract Petal from worrying that we'd be struck by the lightning that was flashing all about. Petal never fretted even *once* about the roaring thunder!

We arrived at the door of the gymnasium, wet and breathless but curiously happy.

Once inside, we shook ourselves like cats coming in out of the rain.

Then, with Ms. Harkness encouraging us, we set about finding things to play with.

At first, we played some indoor soccer. Not because any of us liked soccer—we didn't—but because Mandy kept thinking that Will liked it, and she was trying to get his attention. So we played for fifteen minutes, kicking the ball back and forth.

But then Rebecca reminded Mandy that Will didn't like soccer at all, which caused Mandy to remember that she didn't like soccer either, and so we stopped.

"What do we do now?" Mandy asked.

"Play, children! Play!" Ms. Harkness shouted from the sidelines. She was still holding Petal's little pink umbrella over her head . . . *indoors.*

"There's something not natural about that woman," Mandy muttered as she followed us to the gymnastic equipment, where we climbed all over the uneven bars and the horse thingy, some of us hanging upside down, not caring if our panties were showing. For once, even Annie didn't reprimand us about this. She was too busy hanging upside down herself.

"What do you mean by that?" Jackie asked Mandy. "Why would you say Ms. Harkness doesn't seem natural?"

"Because she doesn't," Mandy said. "Just look at her over there, with that umbrella over her head . . . *indoors.*" She shuddered. "She reminds me of that book *The Cat in the Hat.*"

"What are you talking about?" Rebecca demanded.

"I've always liked that book," Zinnia said, adding, "It's a doozy." But no one seemed to care.

"Those two kids in the book—" Mandy started.

"Sally and her brother," Jackie put in.

"Right," Mandy said. "Those two kids in the book are bored because it's raining out, so when the Cat arrives they're very happy."

"Not entirely," Jackie said. "They are somewhat happy, but they're also concerned, particularly when the Fish gets into the action."

"I've always been fond of the Fish," Petal said wistfully.

"The Fish is a great worrier," Jackie said.

"And rightfully so," Petal added.

"But don't you see?" Mandy said. "Petal is right. The Fish has every good reason to be worried because once the Cat in the Hat comes into the picture, things start to go horribly wrong!"

"But everything turns out all right in the end, doesn't it?" Jackie said.

"But it takes an awful lot of work to get there," Mandy countered. Now she had her hands on her hips. If we hadn't known any better, we'd have sworn this was a new Mandy!

"So what are you saying?" Durinda was puzzled. "Are you saying our teacher is the Cat in the Hat?"

"She's *not* our teacher," Mandy said irritably. "Mrs. McGillicuddy is. This other woman, on the other hand, she's just an . . . impostor!"

We were so stunned at the notion, the *accusation,* we

stopped hanging upside down and things and instead circled around to confront Mandy.

"I don't think so," Annie said. "An impostor is someone who assumes false identity or title for the purpose of deception."

"Ms. Harkness is just a substitute," Marcia said.

"I'm fairly certain no one in the history of the world has ever impersonated a substitute," Durinda said, sounding like Annie.

We all thought for a moment about some of the nasty things we'd done to substitutes over the course of our education. Then we hung our heads in shame. We had been bad.

"Well, I don't think she's like the Cat in the Hat at all," Will piped up. "In fact, I think she's the most amazing teacher of all time! She's like Cinderella or Sleeping Beauty or Snow White or something, but with a shorter skirt."

Normally, we would have been jealous. We would have been jealous that Will, whom we thought of as belonging to *us,* was paying so much attention to a female other than us Eights.

But we couldn't be jealous. As he gazed at her adoringly, so did we all.

Well, except for Mandy.

"I want to be like her when I grow up," Durinda said, a light in her eyes.

"I want to be like her right now," Zinnia said, a light in her eyes too.

"I just wish I hadn't made such a jerk out of myself in front of her," Georgia said glumly.

"What do you mean?" we asked, turning to her.

"Hitting her in the forehead with that spitball," Georgia said. "I can't believe how bad my luck is at times! If I'd thrown that spitball a second earlier, it would have just struck the door; a second later, and I probably would have hit Frank Freud instead. But me, *I* had to throw it at exactly the worst moment possible, when it would hit *her* in the head. Now she shall hate me forever and I will never get a chance to be Teacher's Pet."

We were shocked.

Who would have ever dreamed that Georgia, hard-hearted Georgia, would want to be Teacher's Pet?

We certainly wouldn't have.

But then we all swiveled our heads from Georgia over to Ms. Harkness, who was standing there under Petal's pink umbrella on the sidelines, and we could see her point. We *all* wanted to be Teacher's Pet now.

Well, except for Mandy.

"Georgia," Zinnia said, taking a step forward and placing her hand gently on Georgia's arm.

We were proud of Zinnia in that moment. There were times when she could be as timid as Petal, and Zinnia did worry too much about gifts, but because she was so sensitive herself, she was sometimes the most sensitive to other people. And cats. Well, at least *she* thought so.

"I really don't think Ms. Harkness hates you," Zinnia said once she'd secured Georgia's attention. "Don't you remember? She told you she was going to keep a special eye on you. And she touched your nose. She hasn't touched any of us. In fact, I'd say you're her favorite. I think when she found you on her desk, she was awfully impressed."

It was a long speech for Zinnia to make, and she looked as though she'd exhausted herself. We were proud.

We turned to Georgia to see how she had taken this.

She still looked sad, as though she wasn't wholly convinced and would dearly love to believe Zinnia was right . . . but wasn't sure.

"Or maybe," Rebecca added darkly, "the reason she wants to keep a closer eye on you has nothing to do with being special, at least not in a good way."

"How do you mean?" Georgia asked.

"You know," Rebecca said, "you on the desk? The spitball you hurled at her forehead?"

"I didn't *hurl*—"

"Maybe," Rebecca said, "Ms. Harkness suspects, and

rightfully so, that you're the student most likely to cause trouble."

"I prefer," Georgia said with a sniff, offended, "to believe she wants *me* for Teacher's Pet."

"I still think she's the Cat in the Hat," Mandy maintained, interrupting all our theories about Ms. Harkness and Georgia. "I think she is"—and here Mandy took a huge breath before finishing—"A Bad Person."

"Oh, will you please stop with that?" Georgia demanded, snapping out of her sad and offended mood just long enough to get mad.

"Fine," Mandy said. "I guess I can't help it. I miss Mrs. McGillicuddy."

She *what?* How could anyone possibly miss the McG?

But before we could say this to her, she added, "And I think we should all cheer her up by making her get-well cards."

It seemed like an over-the-top notion at first. Shouldn't getting a break from us cheer up the McG enough? But then we thought about the times when we'd been sick and Mommy and Daddy had bought us get-well cards, even though they lived right in the same house with us. (This was, of course, before they had disappeared. Or died.) Those cards had made us feel good, loved, *better* even, and we could see Mandy's point: cards from us just might be the difference between living and dying for the McG.

So that's what we did when we returned to our classroom after the Longest Recess the Whistle Stop Had Ever Seen *Ever:* we set to work, spending the rest of the day making cards for our absent teacher.

As for our new teacher?

She offered to mail the ten cards for us on her way home. She even offered to spring for the stamps.

* * * * * * * *

"I'm worried about what it will be like when we get home," Petal said as we boarded the bus.

"What are you worried about?" Annie asked. She might have said "What are you worried about *this time?*" That's what Georgia and Rebecca would have said. Even Marcia might have said it on a bad day. But Annie was always the most patient of us with Petal and Zinnia.

"Will our house still be there?" Petal fretted. "It's raining so hard. Maybe it's all under water by now!"

"Don't you remember?" Rebecca pointed out. "We live in a magnificent stone house."

"It's practically a castle!" Zinnia added.

"And it's high on a hill," Jackie said gently. "Water

tends to go downhill, not up, so our house won't be under water."

"Yes," Petal said. "I remember all that now. But do you think the foundation of our house is strong? Because if it's not, with all this rain, and then the wind . . ."

Really, sometimes Petal was a lot to take. We did worry what it would be like when the time came to have her take center stage for a month. She'd probably make us huddle with her under our beds for the entire month of June, never discovering her own power or gift at all.

Poor Petal, we realized as she went on and on. She just couldn't help herself.

It was a good thing then that when we arrived home from school something happened to make Georgia forget about her depression and Petal forget about worrying.

One of the cats was missing.

CHAPTER FIVE

Usually, when we arrived home from school, we found all eight cats waiting for us right inside the door. The cats were hungry or they needed us to clean out the litter boxes for them or maybe they just wanted a good scratch behind their furry ears. Those cats: they were always after something.

But on that day, there were only seven cats there to greet us: Anthrax, Dandruff, Jaguar, Minx, Precious, Rambunctious, and Zither. Greatorex, Georgia's cat, was nowhere in sight.

"Where *is* she?" Georgia cried, concerned.

Even the seven remaining cats looked concerned. They looked frantic too, more frantic than they had looked since the night back in January when our evil neighbor the Wicket had broken into our home and gone through Mommy's private study in search of her Top Secret folder.

"I'll try to get information out of them," Zinnia

offered, referring to the cats, "but it's very hard to talk to them when they get like this."

"Why don't we all change out of our wet things," Annie suggested, "and put on our play clothes? Then we can search."

"But if she were in the house," Georgia said, "then the other cats would have seen her and they wouldn't look so frantic. She must be out there." Georgia looked out through the window. "She must be lost in the monsoon!"

"She will drown for sure," Petal said. "Cats hate rain. Plus, Greatorex doesn't have an ark."

"Will you both stop it?" Rebecca said. She turned on Georgia. "You're beginning to sound as bad as Petal." She turned on Petal. "And you sound as bad as . . . *you!*"

"I'll make hot cocoa for everyone," Durinda offered.

At least she wasn't trying to serve us all tea again.

"It will be fine," Jackie soothed Georgia. "We'll find your cat."

"I don't see any evidence why that should necessarily be true," Marcia said, "but why don't we take Jackie's word for it anyway?"

Normally, the first thing we did after arriving home from school was our homework, because Annie made us, but not on that day. There were two reasons for this: (1) we were all upset about Georgia's cat going missing—although no one was as upset about it as

Georgia—because it reminded us of the night our parents disappeared, or died; and (2) Ms. Harkness, beautiful Ms. Harkness, hadn't assigned any.

So we all changed out of our wet things and into our play clothes and had some cocoa in the dining room.

By that point, the seven remaining cats had settled down a bit. In fact, Rambunctious had settled down so much, she was snoozing in the center of the table, her long tail circling around Rebecca's empty cocoa cup.

It was then, just as everyone was starting to breathe a little easier—if for no other reason than that we were all dry and we'd drank something warm—that we heard a crash coming from the kitchen.

"That's odd," Durinda said, jumping up to go see what had fallen down. We all followed her.

In the kitchen, Carl the talking refrigerator and robot Betty were flirting again. This had been going on ever since Pete the mechanic had helped them work out their romantic differences, back in February. Seeing them together like that sometimes made us think, *Eeew, gross,* but mostly it just made us happy.

It was no use asking Carl and Betty about the source of the noise—they were too wrapped up in each other—but anyway, we could see it for ourselves.

Somehow, the huge tin of dried cocoa had been knocked out of the cabinet. The lid was off, cocoa was spilled all over the floor, and in the center of the cocoa were a few tiny paw prints.

"Now, how did that happen?" Durinda wondered aloud. "I'm sure I put that tin far back in the cabinet. I don't see how it could have fallen out on its own."

"And look at those paw prints," Marcia said. "All seven of the remaining cats were in the dining room with us. They couldn't have made those prints."

"Look!" Georgia shouted.

We looked.

And as we looked, we saw little strips of dried cocoa disappear from the spillage on the floor. It was as though a tiny, invisible tongue were licking it up.

"What's going on here?" Annie demanded.

The cocoa stopped disappearing at once. As we looked, little cocoa prints in the shape of tiny paws appeared on the floor. We watched as the cocoa paw prints made their way to the door. We followed the cocoa paw prints, which kept getting fainter, until we reached the cat room.

The cat room was like our drawing room, a place to hang out, but for cats.

We stood in the doorway waiting to see what would happen next. It was tough to know what was going on because the cocoa paw prints had faded into nothing.

Then we heard a sound:

Lap, lap, lap.

We followed the sound with our eyes, and our gaze arrived at Zither's water dish. We could tell it was hers because all the cats had their names on their water dishes: Daddy's doing. He had such nice handwriting.

All the other water dishes were empty. We listened to that sound of *lap, lap, lap,* watching as the water line on Zither's dish dipped lower and lower, the water sloshing a bit with each *lap* sound.

"What *is* going on here?" Annie asked again.

"Just a moment," Zinnia said, holding up a finger and acting as if she actually expected us to obey her while she crouched down and whispered something in Zither's ear. Then Zinnia held her own ear to Zither's mouth, as though listening.

A moment later, as promised, Zinnia was back on her feet. And she had a report for us.

"That's Greatorex," Zinnia said, indicating with a

jut of her chin the invisible space above Zither's water dish.

"*What?*" Rebecca said. "What are you talking about now, you silly child?"

"It's true," Zinnia said with rare firmness. "Zither says Greatorex has somehow figured out how to make herself disappear."

"*What?*" Georgia said. If anything, Georgia sounded more outraged than Rebecca had.

Zinnia went on as though Georgia hadn't spoken. "Zither says," Zinnia said, "that all day, ever since Greatorex figured out this trick, she's been tormenting them with it. She steals their food, their water. She bumps them out of the way whenever she pleases, and they can't bump her back because they can't see her. She even sneaks off with all the best toys."

As if to illustrate this last point, there was a *thump* in the area of a high counter. A moment later, there was a *bat* sound, followed by a ball of purple yarn sailing right over our heads. Annie, the tallest, had to duck a bit.

"I don't believe it," Jackie said. "Or, I should say, I *wouldn't* believe it if I wasn't *not* seeing it with my very own eyes. I think Zinnia's right!"

"You know," Marcia observed, "I've heard people say before that ours is a crazy house, and I have to say now: I'm beginning to believe them!"

"Is anyone else thinking what I'm thinking?" Petal said.

"I doubt it," Rebecca said with a sneer.

Petal ignored her. "It's just that," Petal said, "Annie's power is that she can be as smart as an adult. Then, right after she discovered her power, we all noticed that Anthrax was getting bossier with the other cats. Er, I mean smarter," Petal hastily added, having caught the look on Annie's face. She went on. "Durinda discovers she can make people—except Zinnia—freeze by tapping her leg three times rapidly and then pointing her finger. Suddenly, Dandruff is doing the same thing, making the other cats freeze—except for Zither, of course. Now Greatorex discovers, *somehow,* that she can make herself disappear." She paused. "Do you see what I'm getting at?"

It was shocking, to think that Petal was capable of making such an important point. And yet she had.

Seven heads swiveled to stare at Georgia.

"What?" Georgia said, perplexed. "What is everyone staring at me for?" Then a look of horror dawned on her face. "Oh, no!" she cried. "I don't believe it! This is so unfair! First, my gift arrives, borne under the wing of a carrier pigeon, but it's too early, so I send it away. And now my power—*my power!*—appears in my *cat* before it appears in me?"

We had to admit: things weren't exactly working out

for Georgia according to the usual plan. If we were her, we thought, we'd be upset too.

"Aargh!" Georgia shouted. "I have the worst luck of anybody!"

* * * * * * * *

We retired to Winter to calm down.

Winter was one of the four seasonal rooms at the back of the house that Mommy had created so we could go to whichever season we wanted. True, we should have been sick of the cold, but the rains of March were making us long for the pure whiteness of fresh snow. We did have to put on our parkas and snowshoes to go to Winter, but the man-made snow on the ground there, and the hills, and the great big sled, made it worth it.

We dragged in a table upon which to set our drinks, as well as chairs to sit in while we drank.

After we'd gotten Georgia calmed down—more cocoa would have been in order, but it had all been spilled on the kitchen floor and was dirty, so we had settled for a round of juice boxes instead—she had some practical questions.

"But how did Greatorex make herself disappear?" she asked. "And, more important, can she make herself come back again?"

"She's your cat," Zinnia pointed out. "Why don't you just ask her?"

Georgia made a face at Zinnia. We all did.

"Fine," Zinnia said. "Then you, as her mistress, command her to reappear, and *I'll* ask her."

Georgia sighed. "I suppose," she said, "it's worth a shot." Then, in a much louder voice: "Greatorex, I *order* you to reappear!"

In an instant, Greatorex was among us again. She leaped into Georgia's lap, and as Georgia petted her, she looked greatly relieved—Georgia, not the cat.

We could understand this. Georgia had probably been worried that she'd never see her cat again. It would have been awful to be the only girl in our house without her own cat.

Zinnia leaned over and whispered in Greatorex's ear.

Greatorex shook her head, keeping her mouth firmly shut.

"Fine," Zinnia said, loud enough for us to hear. "Then I'll ask Zither. Zither!"

Zither came bounding through the snow to Zinnia.

More whispering ensued.

We didn't really believe that Zinnia could understand the cats, or they her, but Zinnia did come up with the most astounding things.

At last, Zinnia spoke. "Zither says that Greatorex makes herself disappear by twitching her nose back and forth two times."

"I'd try that," Georgia said dryly, "but how would I ever make myself come back?"

"Zither says," Zinnia said, "that she's not completely certain, but she thinks that Greatorex reappears the same way."

"That sounds like a rather iffy proposition," Georgia said.

"Try it!" Jackie said.

"Try it!" Marcia said.

"What have you got to lose?" Rebecca sneered.

"Oh, I don't know," Georgia said. "My whole body?" But then, in an act of amazing bravery, Georgia twitched her nose twice.

In an instant, she was gone, leaving Greatorex suspended in thin air about six inches above the chair in which Georgia had been sitting with the cat

in her lap. Then the cat leaped to the snowy floor. Three seconds later, Jackie felt a poke on her shoulder.

"It's me," we heard Georgia say.

Two seconds after that, Annie felt a tickle between her ribs.

"That was me too," we heard Georgia say. "I thought you could use a good laugh."

A full minute later, a can of pink frosting and a silver spoon came floating into the room; they landed on the table right in front of Rebecca.

"I thought," we heard Georgia say, "a little pink frosting might improve your mood."

And then, almost immediately, Georgia was with us again: her whole body and not just her voice.

"How did you do all that?" Durinda asked, awed.

"The double nose-twitch," Georgia said calmly, as though she'd been doing it her whole life. "It really does work, and it works both ways."

Then Georgia found Greatorex under a chair and gave her a good scratch beneath the chin. "Thanks, Greatorex. I don't know if I could have figured it out without you. But please stop tormenting the other cats."

"Hey," Rebecca said, "does anyone see what I see? Georgia must be just as crazy as Zinnia! She's talking to her cat as if she expects the cat to understand her."

"Maybe she can," Georgia said with a shrug.

"Oh, I'm worried," Petal said. "I am very worried now."

"About what?" Jackie asked kindly.

"What if Georgia makes herself disappear in the middle of the night?" Petal worried aloud. "What if she comes into my bedroom and starts pinching me in the dark and I can't see her? It will frighten me."

"I promise I won't do that," Georgia said. It was as if she'd somehow grown older that afternoon. "A power is a great responsibility. I promise not to abuse mine." Then a gleam entered her eye. "But you never know. At the right time, in the right place, being able to make yourself disappear and then appear again could come in handy."

Later that night, before going to bed, we remembered to check behind the loose stone in the wall in the drawing room. This time, the note there was the right note.

Dear Georgia,

Nice work . . . finally! Five down, eleven to go.

A half-hour afterward, even though we couldn't all see it, we were sure Georgia went to sleep with a smile on her face.

CHAPTER SIX

It was one week later, so it was Monday again, the same day repeating itself being what happens when an entire week goes by.

In the seven days that had passed since the last time it was Monday, Georgia had spent many hours practicing her new power. The rains hadn't completely stopped yet, and water did still trickle down  from the sky. This meant that when Georgia went down to get the mail each day, invisible, we could see her umbrella bob its way down the hill and bob back up again with a stack of mail floating in the air below it. We all thought this looked very funny, but Annie put a stop to it.

"What if the mailperson sees that mail floating with no body there to carry it?" Annie said. "It could give him a worse fright than the time Rebecca locked Rambunctious in the mailbox in order to see what mailperson and cat would do when mailperson opened box and cat leaped out at mailperson."

She made a good point. Regarding the mailperson and the cat, as Mommy always said, "It's always funny until someone starts to cry."

"You probably don't need me to remind you of this," Annie reminded Georgia before school that Monday, "but you have to be careful about when and where you practice your make-yourself-invisible trick. It wouldn't do to suddenly disappear in front of Mandy's eyes or to suddenly reappear in a spot where you're not supposed to be."

All the way in on the bus, we worried that Annie's warnings were falling on deaf Georgia ears, but when we got to our classroom, the only person who had disappeared that was supposed to be there was the McG.

Our regular teacher was still absent.

But that was okay! Because there was Serena Harkness, floating into our classroom on her usual sea of beauty.

Mandy's hand shot up.

"Yes, Mandy?" Ms. Harkness said.

"Is Mrs. McGillicuddy still sick?" Mandy asked.

"Obviously," Ms. Harkness said. "Why else would I be here?"

"But it's been such a long time," Mandy said. "It's been a whole week!"

"Don't you like me?" Ms. Harkness asked sweetly.

We all looked at Mandy, wondering what she'd say. We knew for a fact that Mandy didn't like Ms. Harkness, that Mandy thought Ms. Harkness was A Bad Person, but Mandy never told lies. So what would she say now?

"That's not the point," Mandy said.

Nice side step! we thought.

"A week is a long time for a teacher to be absent," Mandy went on.

"But when Principal Freud introduced me, he told you she might be gone that long, even longer," Ms. Harkness countered.

"Yes," Mandy said. "But we all wrote Mrs. McGillicuddy those get-well cards, and you sent them for us. And yet we haven't received any thank-you notes in reply. I think it is all very odd. Cards are very important to Mrs. McGillicuddy—I know this for a fact, and I'm sure she would have replied to ours by now."

"Perhaps," Ms. Harkness said, "she is too sick to write."

Did we just see Ms. Harkness's candy-apple lip curl as she said that last thing to Mandy? Well, we could hardly blame her. Mandy did have that effect on people.

"I'm sure you'll hear from her just as soon as she's feeling well enough," Ms. Harkness added, her usual sweet tone back in place. Then, before Mandy could say any more annoying things, Ms. Harkness clapped her hands together. "Today is March tenth," she said, "yes?"

We all shot our hands up.

"Yes." Ms. Harkness answered her own question without giving us a chance. "And that means that just one week from today, there will be a very important holiday. Can anyone tell me what that holiday is?"

"St. Patrick's Day!" Will shouted without raising his hand.

"Very good, Will," Ms. Harkness said.

"I didn't know St. Patrick's Day was an important holiday," Mandy said. She was puzzled. Then she looked sad. "But I'm sure that if Mrs. McGillicuddy was here, she'd enjoy it."

Ms. Harkness ignored Mandy. We could understand why.

"I'll bet you all like holidays," Ms. Harkness said.

Yes and no, we thought.

We always used to love holidays. And we had enjoyed Valentine's Day back in February. That's when we realized that Will loved all of us just as much as we loved him, plus it had been nice when Carl the talking refrigerator's romance with robot Betty had begun. But we'd been stranded by a snowstorm last Christmas and then our parents had disappeared—or died—on New Year's Eve, so we knew that a holiday could turn on a person without notice.

But we couldn't tell Ms. Harkness all of that, so for once, we kept silent.

"What do you normally do here at the Whistle Stop to celebrate St. Patrick's Day?" Ms. Harkness asked.

"Do?" Mandy was puzzled again. "If it falls during the week, we come to school. I mean, it's not like it's Christmas or Thanksgiving or anything."

Ms. Harkness looked shocked. "You mean you've never had a St. Patrick's Day parade in school before?" she asked.

"No," Zinnia said, her eyes going round as saucers. "But we would like one. A parade is almost as good as getting presents."

"I'm glad you feel that way," Ms. Harkness said. "Because this year, the Whistle Stop *is* going to have a parade! And guess what else."

We all leaned forward.

"The third grade is going to lead the parade," Ms. Harkness said.

This truly was amazing news! The Whistle Stop ran from kindergarten through twelfth grade, and yet we would be marching ahead of the whole school!

"Will this all be in the Tuesday folders?" Mandy asked without raising her hand. "You never sent Tuesday folders home last week. Tuesday folders are red and contain Important Papers. Will you be sending Tuesday folders home this week?"

"No," Ms. Harkness said. "Why would I do that when I can just tell you and then you can tell your parents?"

Mandy's jaw dropped. This, to Mandy, was chaos.

"Now, do you know what else?" Ms. Harkness asked.

We couldn't imagine, but we were very eager to learn.

"Georgia," Ms. Harkness announced, "is going to be Grand Marshal!"

"Congratulations!" we all cried, and we gathered around Georgia to give her high-fives.

Georgia looked very proud, as well she might. Then:

"But what does the Grand Marshal do?" Georgia asked.

"Why, she walks ahead of everyone else," Ms. Harkness said, "and she carries the biggest flag of all."

We thought Georgia might faint dead away from the sheer thrill of it all.

Ms. Harkness clapped her pretty hands once more.

"Now, everyone get your raincoats on and we can head over to the gymnasium. You can practice your marching and flag-carrying, so you'll all be ready for next Monday's parade."

"But surely Mrs. McGillicuddy will be back by next Monday," Mandy objected.

"She might be," Ms. Harkness said. "But then again, she might not."

"But what if it's still raining next Monday?"

Mandy could be such a pest.

"Oh, I'm sure the rain will stop for that one day," Ms. Harkness said.

And somehow, we were all convinced that even the weather couldn't say no to Serena Harkness.

* * * * * * * *

In the gymnasium, we were all very excited to get our flags and our marching assignments. Georgia's flag really was the biggest, and she put the *grand* in Grand Marshal, marching up ahead of us.

Almost a minute into the marching, Georgia stopped and turned around.

"Do you think Ms. Harkness made me Grand Marshal," she said, whispering so our substitute teacher couldn't hear her, "because she thinks I'm special or impressive, like Zinnia said?" She looked worried. "Or is it because of what Rebecca said, that she thinks I'm trouble and if I'm at the head of the line it's easier to keep an eye on me?"

"Who cares why?" Annie whispered back before Rebecca could whisper anything nasty; Rebecca's mouth had opened. "I think you should just enjoy your moment in the sun."

So that's what Georgia did. We all did.

We marched up and down the length of the gym, with Ms. Harkness watching from the sidelines.

About five minutes into our marching, Ms. Harkness pulled out a cell phone and started talking on it.

"That's odd," Mandy muttered. "Mrs. McGillicuddy never talks on her phone when she's supposed to be watching us."

"Well," Rebecca pointed out with a sneer, "it's not as though we can hurt ourselves just marching with flags."

"I need to go to the bathroom," Georgia suddenly announced. "Here, Zinnia, take this big flag for me. You lead for a bit."

Before any of us could object, Georgia walked off toward the door that led to the girls' locker room.

Zinnia was the smallest of us, a full seven inches shorter than Annie. The huge flag nearly toppled her, but she did seem very proud, marching ahead of us.

We marched on.

Georgia was gone at least ten minutes. By the time she returned, Ms. Harkness had ended her phone call, told us all that we had earned a break from marching, and announced recess. When Georgia strolled up to us, we were all hanging upside down on the gymnastic equipment.

"Don't you have to go to the bathroom too?" Georgia said to Mandy.

"No," Mandy said. "I went before I came to school."

"That's funny," Georgia said. "Just looking at you, I was very sure that you must have to go."

A look of horror came over Mandy's face.

"Oh, no!" she cried. "Suddenly I do!"

And she ran off toward the girls' locker room.

"Gather round," Georgia whispered in an urgent voice once Mandy was gone.

"No," Rebecca said. "It's too much fun hanging upside down."

"All the blood is rushing to our heads," Marcia observed.

"And it feels really good," Durinda said. "It beats cooking meals for eight."

We knew that despite the praise it earned her, Durinda sometimes resented being our cook.

"Fine," Georgia said, "then I'll just have to talk to you like that. There's not much time."

"What are you talking about?" Annie said.

"I think Mandy is right," Georgia said darkly.

"I don't think anyone has said 'Mandy is right' in the history of the world," Annie said. "And right about what?"

"Do you think my brains will pour out of my ears if I keep hanging upside down like this?" Petal asked.

Petal's face was getting very red.

"When I went to the bathroom," Georgia said, "I didn't really go to the bathroom."

"Then why did you go there?" Jackie asked.

"I mean," Georgia went on, "I did go into the bathroom, but once inside, I made myself invisible. Then I came back out again, still invisible, and tiptoed over to Ms. Harkness."

"But why did you do that?" Zinnia asked.

"I don't know." Georgia shrugged, as though she hadn't had a good reason. "Because I could."

"Wow," Marcia said. "Like climbing Mount Everest."

"And what did you learn?" Annie asked. "What did you learn that made you say 'Mandy is right'?"

"I didn't say 'Mandy is right,'" Georgia corrected. "I said 'I *think* Mandy is right.'"

"Hairsplitting." Rebecca yawned. "I knew you hadn't really discovered anything."

We all knew that Rebecca was jealous that she didn't have any special power yet. Or gift.

Georgia ignored Rebecca.

"I heard Ms. Harkness whispering into her phone," Georgia said. "I heard her saying to the person at the other end, 'I don't think they're as smart as you warned me they were. In fact, they don't seem very bright at all, F—'"

"So what does that mean?" Rebecca demanded. "And what is *F*—?"

"I'm not completely sure," Georgia admitted. "I got spooked that she might somehow hear me breathing, so I ran off. But something about the way she said it, I had this awful feeling that she was talking about us."

We all laughed at her, even Will, who never laughed at anybody.

"Never mind 'I think Mandy is right.'" Now even Annie was scoffing. "I'm beginning to think you should be saying 'I think that I, Georgia, am turning into Mandy'!"

"Why don't you hang upside down for a while," Rebecca suggested. "Maybe that will help you get your head back on straight."

Georgia opened her mouth to object, but then Mandy returned and all talk of whether Mandy was right or not ceased.

* * * * * * * *

So that's how we passed the week: practicing our marching in the gym. This was our second full week without any homework. You would think we would be happy about this fact, but . . .

"I don't like it," Annie said, "never having any homework anymore. I mean, our parents are paying a lot of money for our education. Shouldn't we be getting one?"

CHAPTER SEVEN

Parade day!

It was Monday, March 17, and we were all so excited, we woke up a full hour early.

The Whistle Stop had never had a St. Patrick's Day parade before, but we were going to have one now.

We brushed our teeth and hair, rushed into our school clothes, and zipped downstairs for breakfast without Annie having to urge us to "Hurry it along!" even once.

But then, while we ate our pancakes, a sadness fell over the room.

"What's wrong with all of you?" Annie asked. "You should be so happy today."

"I know," Petal said, "but we've heard the other kids at school talking. Everyone else will have at least one parent there to watch the parade today."

"Oh," Annie said. "That is hard."

It was. We didn't want to be the only kids at the parade without anyone there to cheer for us, with no one but one another to be proud.

"Say," Annie said. "I have an idea. Come on!"

She rose from the table and we followed where she led: right to Mommy's private study.

We normally didn't like to go into Mommy's study unless it was an absolute emergency. Mommy had had a rule that we couldn't go in there, and we still tried to obey the rule even now that she'd gone to . . . wherever she had gone to.

"What are you doing?" Durinda asked as Annie seated herself behind Mommy's desk and picked up the phone.

"I found this phone's instruction manual," Annie said, "and I realized it's also a speakerphone. It's the only one in the house that is."

Annie dialed a number and hit a button on the phone, and we listened as the phone of whomever she was calling started to ring.

"Who are you calling?" Jackie asked.

"Shh," Annie said as we heard a click; someone had picked up at the other end.

"Hullo," a man's sleepy voice said.

It was Pete the mechanic!

"Mr. Pete, this is Annie Huit," Annie said.

"Oh, hullo, Annie!" Pete sounded wide awake now. And somehow he seemed both cheerful and concerned. "You don't need your car fixed this early in the morning, do you, lamb? You haven't been sabotaged again?"

"Oh, no," Annie said hurriedly, "nothing like that. We were just wondering . . ." Suddenly, Annie sounded shy.

"Yes, Annie? How can I help?"

Annie spoke in a rush, as though worried that she'd lose her nerve if she didn't. "It's just that, at our school today there's going to be a big parade, for St. Patrick's Day, and we're going to be marching in it, and all of the other kids will have at least one parent there . . ." She ran out of steam as a sad expression came over her face. "Of course, it's a Monday, so you'll no doubt be working at Pete's Repairs and Auto Wrecking . . ."

"I do usually work Mondays," he said gently.

"Yes," Annie said, more sadly yet, "I did just realize that."

"What time did you say the parade was?" Pete asked.

"I didn't," Annie said. "But it's at two o'clock. It'll take up the whole hour before school ends. Of course, that's still in the middle of your workday, so—"

"I'll be there with bells on," Pete said.

We had no idea what that meant exactly, but it did sound good.

"I'm afraid Mrs. Pete won't be able to make it," Pete added. "She's off visiting her sister. But I'll be there—"

"Yes, with bells on!" Annie said excitedly.

"—because you can always count on me." Pete finished making his point. "I'd be honored to be your loco parentis."

We thought that maybe Pete was calling our parents crazy. But that didn't sound like something Pete would say.

"Thank you, Mr. Pete!" eight voices shouted into the speakerphone.

"No," Pete said right back at us. "Thank *you,* Eights."

We sighed happy sighs as Annie switched off the speakerphone. It was tough sometimes to know whom we loved more in our world: Will or Mr. Pete.

Back at the breakfast table, we all finished our pancakes with relish. All except Georgia, that is.

Georgia wasn't eating at all.

"I'm afraid I'm not going today," Georgia said.

"Not going!" Jackie cried. "But how can you miss the parade?"

"Aren't you feeling well?" Durinda asked.

"Yes and no," Georgia said. "My body feels okay enough. It's just that . . . this month! Everything has been about luck! What good luck: my gift arrives early.

What bad luck: I send it away. What good luck: my cat discovers my power. What bad luck: my cat discovers my power before I do. What good luck: I get named Grand Marshal. What bad luck: I can't go."

"Yes," Annie said, "I do see that you've developed a theme there. But I still don't understand that last part. Why can't you go?"

"Because I feel funny about it," Georgia said, "and for once, I'm going to try to get things right."

"So what will you do instead?" Marcia asked. "Stay home?"

"Stay home alone," Rebecca said, "on what will probably be the most fun day we'll ever have at school?"

"I should get very lonely if I stayed home alone," Petal said. "I'd be scared too."

"No," Georgia said. "I guess I shouldn't have said before that I'm not going. I am still going . . . only I'm going to be invisible. That means that you, Annie, need to do your Daddy impersonation in order to phone me in sick."

"I still don't understand," Annie said.

"I'm not sure that I fully understand either," Georgia said. "But it's what I want."

"Very well," Annie said.

"Just don't go around pinching me all day while you're busy being invisible," Petal said.

"But wait a second," Zinnia said. "If you're not going

to be Grand Marshal—which you can't be if you're busy being invisible—then who will lead the parade?"

"You will," Georgia said, placing her hand on Zinnia's shoulder. "You're the only one besides me who's had any practice at it."

* * * * * * * *

Pete didn't have any bells on, at least not that we could see, nor did he have on the Armani tuxedo jacket he'd worn that one time he'd bailed us out of trouble with Principal Freud and the McG. He just had on his navy blue mechanic's T-shirt and his loose jeans that hung down below his big belly. It didn't matter what he wore, though. We were just so glad to see him as we paraded on past, his salt-and-pepper hair shining in the sun as though he'd used conditioner just for us. We were so happy to see the look of pride in his dancing blue eyes as he put his fingers to his lips, let out a long whistle, and then screamed, "Go, Eights!"

Right before the festivities had started, we introduced Mandy to Pete. We hadn't really wanted to, but she'd been just standing there when he arrived in his pickup. So we'd told her what we'd gotten in the habit of telling everybody: that Pete was our uncle. Pete didn't seem to mind, and Mandy seemed oddly impressed that we had an uncle who wore his jeans so low.

It was a beautiful day for a parade.

The weather, as Ms. Harkness had promised, was cooperating. The last trickles of rain had finally ended sometime in the night, and a powerful sun hung over the Whistle Stop. Zinnia, filling in for Georgia as Grand Marshal, led the entire student body around the school grounds.

Zinnia bobbed up ahead of us. Occasionally, the large flag she carried veered off to one side, threatening to pull her over with it, but then the flag would straighten up as though helped by some invisible force.

We knew what that invisible force was: Georgia.

"This is great," Marcia said as we marched.

"I feel as though we're part of a marching band," Jackie said.

"I feel as though we're marching off to war," Rebecca said with a gleam in her eye.

We all suspected Rebecca would enjoy a war.

"Are you sure we should be doing this?" fretted Petal.

"What do you mean?" asked Durinda.

"Aren't we Jewish?" Petal asked. "It's what Jackie always says."

"Who knows?" Annie shrugged. "It's been a while since we were in a church or a synagogue." She thought a moment before adding, "Or a mosque."

"But this is a St. Patrick's Day parade," Petal insisted. "Are we even Irish?"

"With a name like Huit?" Annie gave another shrug. "I don't think so. But I can't see any harm in marching."

So on we marched.

Zinnia said nothing. She was too busy trying to keep that flag aloft.

And then, all too soon, the hour was up, the parade was over, our day in the sun was finished. We said goodbye to Pete, who had to rush back to work.

We watched as most of the other students went off with their parents. Then we headed back to the classroom. If we hurried, we could just make our bus.

"Where are you seven going?" We were stopped by the voice of Serena Harkness.

"We need to get our things from the classroom," Annie told her. "Then we have to hurry to catch the bus."

"Oh, dear." Ms. Harkness put a pretty hand to her own pretty cheek. "Do you mean you didn't have even one parent here to see you today? You don't have even one parent to take you home?"

Seven visible heads plus one invisible one shook no.

"Our father is modeling in France," Jackie said.

"Mommy went with him this time," said Zinnia.

"But our uncle will be by later to check on us," Annie hastily added so Ms. Harkness wouldn't worry that we'd be home alone.

"But what about Georgia?" Ms. Harkness asked. "Who's taking care of her? You know, I really do worry about her whenever I can't see her."

"Ouch!" Annie said, and we realized that Georgia must have pinched her between the ribs. "That's right. Er, our aunt is there with her right now. Aunt, er, Sally."

"I tell you what," Ms. Harkness said as though she'd just had the most wonderful idea. "Why don't *I* give you a ride home today?"

"How big is your car?" Rebecca asked. "There are eight of us here, you know. Ouch! I mean seven."

"We fill up most of the minibus," Marcia added.

"Oh," Ms. Harkness said, "I have a vehicle big enough to hold all of you. Come along."

So we followed her to the teachers' parking lot, where, it turned out, she *did* have a big vehicle.

"I think that must be the biggest car ever made!" Zinnia said, awe in her eyes. The vehicle was huge, and it was painted the color of an army uniform.

"Do you like it?" Ms. Harkness asked. "I just bought it yesterday."

When we climbed inside of it, it did have that new-car smell.

Ms. Harkness put the key in the ignition, and the car hummed to life. Then she pulled out of the parking lot and onto the street.

"Don't you need me to tell you where to go?" Annie yelled from the back.

"I have an even better idea," Ms. Harkness said as she drove, speaking as though this idea too had just come to her. "Why don't I take you all back to my place for dinner? With your parents both in France, your aunt taking care of Georgia, and your uncle not stopping by until later, it might be more fun for you. I know—we can even order a pizza!"

Seven voices instantly shouted, "Yes!"

Georgia pinched us all at least five times, but it was too late: we'd already accepted the invitation.

And we were glad we had.

After all, what could be better than being invited over to have pizza with Serena Harkness?

CHAPTER EIGHT

The house was solid brick; at least, the whole front side of it was, with not a window in sight.

For some reason, we all thought immediately of the last house that was built by the Three Little Pigs—you know, the one the wolf couldn't blow down.

The house was also very large, even larger than our house!

And it was the only house on the street.

"Wow," Rebecca whispered, then she let out a low whistle. "I had no idea substitute teachers made so much money."

"Come along," Ms. Harkness chirruped at us. Then she used several keys to open the several locks that were on the one iron door that was the only way into the house as far as the eye could see.

Once we were inside, she locked just as many locks from the inside before pocketing the set of keys.

"Feel free to look around," she said, turning on the lights. "I just need to check on something in the other room. Won't be more than a few minutes, and then we can order that pizza."

Since it's silly to refuse an invitation to be nosy, we took her at her word and looked around.

The front room was the most beautiful room we'd ever been in. Everything was a work of art, and yet so touchable, in pretty shades of pink and purple, green and turquoise.

"Psst," we heard Georgia's voice hiss. "Get out of this house while you still can. Something's not right here."

But we ignored her voice. We even ignored all her pinches.

We'd seen the Wicket's house. We knew what evil looked like, and this wasn't it.

There was a painting on the wall, a very large painting of two women, obviously twins, with long chestnut-colored hair. The women reminded us of Serena Harkness, but they were about ten years older than her. They also reminded us of someone else, but we couldn't quite figure out of whom. One of the women's eyes were chocolate brown; the other woman's eyes looked as if they were moving around desperately.

Huh. That was funny. Those moving eyes that were following us about, they looked like the McG's eyes.

But as we stepped toward the painting, thinking to investigate further, Ms. Harkness returned.

Something about her had changed in the short time she'd been out of the room. Not her clothes, not her hair—it was nothing like that. Rather, it was the way she acted toward us.

"Come along now," she said, but it wasn't in the bright and friendly way she'd said it before. "Don't dawdle."

Feeling as though we couldn't argue, we followed her out of that room, around the corner, and into another room.

This room was nothing like the front room.

The walls were made of dark brick, and there were no windows, although we supposed, having seen the front of the house, we shouldn't have expected any. It was like a dungeon except it wasn't in a basement. The floor was made of cold-looking cement, and there wasn't a stick of furniture or a pillow or a decoration or a painting in sight. But there *was* one other person, and we don't mean Ms. Harkness, and we don't mean Invisible Georgia.

"McG!" we cried, unable to address our teacher properly in the midst of our shock.

"Eights!" she cried back at us, equally shocked.

And what was even more shocking? The McG actually looked relieved to see us.

"What's going on here?" Annie demanded, rounding on Ms. Harkness.

"Isn't it obvious?" Ms. Harkness said. "And I was informed that you eight—now seven—were supposed to be so very smart. Well, from where I'm sitting, you don't seem very smart at all."

"You're not sitting," Rebecca pointed out. "You're standing."

It probably wasn't the best time for rudeness, but we couldn't blame Rebecca. And, truth be told, if we hadn't been so scared right then, we would have cheered for her.

"Fine." Ms. Harkness bit off the word. "I'm not sitting. But I still can't believe you can't figure this out."

"You kidnapped our teacher," Annie said.

"Yes," Ms. Harkness admitted freely.

"Then you impersonated a substitute teacher," Durinda said.

"Yes again," Ms. Harkness said.

It would normally have been Georgia's turn to speak, but she was too busy being invisible.

"You staged the St. Patrick's Day parade for a purpose," Jackie said.

"So you could lure us here afterward," Marcia said.

"I don't like you anymore," Petal said, her lower lip starting to quiver.

"Now I'm not sure why I ever did," said Rebecca.

"I wish I'd never carried that stupid flag," said Zinnia.

"This isn't getting us anywhere," Ms. Harkness said. "You still haven't told me *why* I would do all this."

And we still didn't know. We did have our theories. But if we voiced those theories, we might be giving away information best kept secret . . . *Top* Secret.

"Fine," Ms. Harkness said when it became obvious that we wouldn't speak anymore. "I know all about your mother being a scientist. Believe me, I know *a lot* about your dear mother."

How dare she talk about Mommy as though she knew her!

"And I know about that project your mother was working on," Ms. Harkness went on. "I don't know all the details, but I know it involves the secret of eternal life."

Her eyes looked kind of crazy when she said that last part. It was amazing, we were beginning to realize, how crazy certain adults got when the subject of the secret of eternal life came up.

"I want to know what you know," Ms. Harkness said. "I want you to tell me where your mother is. *I want that secret!*"

But we remained silent. We remained silent because (1) we really didn't have the answers she wanted—we knew very little, other than that our parents had both disappeared, or died; and (2) we wouldn't have told her anything even if we *did* know. She was obviously a crazy lady, and who knew what would happen if such Top Secret information fell into the wrong hands? She was so crazy, she probably imagined herself taking over the world.

"So that's the way it's going to be, then?" Serena Harkness said, crossing her arms across her chest as she tapped one high-heeled foot in anger. "You're just going to keep everything to yourselves? Well, if that's the way you want to play it"—and here she turned on her heel and started striding to the door—"I'll lock you in until you get so hungry, you'll beg me to let you talk! I'll tell you one thing before I go, though: I'm glad that pesky Georgia isn't here. She always was the most trouble of you Eights!"

Then she left the room, and we heard the door lock behind her.

We looked at the McG. The McG looked at us.

Then something happened that we never could have imagined happening, not in a million years.

The McG opened up her arms wide and held them toward us.

"Oh, Eights!" she said, somehow hugging all of us at once. "I'm so sorry we're all in this mess, but I've never been so happy to see anyone in my whole life! I've been so lonely here these past two weeks!"

It felt good to be hugged by an adult, even if that adult was the McG. Plus, we did feel responsible in a way; after all, Crazy Serena had kidnapped her over something having to do with *our* family.

But no sooner did we settle into enjoying the group hug than:

"We've been kidnapped!" Petal cried, looking at the locked door.

"Never mind kidnapped," Annie said, and even she looked scared now. "We've been *eightnapped!*"

"I just noticed something," the McG said soothingly,

perhaps hoping to calm our growing mass hysteria. She started counting heads. "There are only seven of you here. Where in the world is Georgia?"

"Georgia," seven voices whispered, much to the McG's astonishment. "Georgia, are you in here?"

But there was no answering whisper, nor were there any pinches.

It was then we realized that when Crazy Serena had exited the room, Invisible Georgia had somehow managed to sneak out with her.

We hoped that wherever Georgia was, she was safe.

And, we realized with a strange sense of relief, at least one of us would survive to tell the tale.

CHAPTER NINE

In that house, the minutes and hours dragged on, and we didn't know if it was day or night.

We grew hungry, we grew thirsty, we grew *bored*.

We could only hope that wherever Georgia was, she really was safe.

"She probably found a TV to watch and is watching it with the sound off," Zinnia said.

"She probably snuck into the kitchen and is having a feast," Petal grumbled. "I'm *so* hungry."

"She probably found a can of pink frosting," Rebecca said, "and she's eating the whole thing herself."

"This isn't getting us anywhere," Annie said.

"Annie's right," Durinda said. "Let's focus on the positive."

"Such as?" Rebecca asked, hands on hips.

"Well, when none of us shows up for school tomorrow, and Crazy Serena—" Jackie began, referring to our captor as we'd begun to think of her, but the McG cut her off.

"You mustn't refer to her that way," our teacher said.

"Why not?" Jackie asked.

"Because she's a teacher," the McG said.

"Oh, is she really?" Rebecca demanded, hands on hips again. "I'm not so sure of that."

"And she is crazy," Marcia observed.

"Plus," Jackie said, "we reserve terms of respect—Mr., Mrs., Miss, Ms.—for people we actually feel respect *for*."

"Yes," Petal said, "like Mr. Pete."

"But isn't that man your uncle?" The McG was puzzled. "So why would you call him *Mr.?*"

"Never mind that now," Annie said.

"And didn't you all shout 'McG!' when you first saw me here, without any *Mrs.* before it?"

She was obviously worried that we didn't respect her, and none of us wanted her to know that the jury was still out on that, so Durinda hurriedly said, "We meant it friendly-like." Then she nodded. "You were saying, Jackie?"

"I was saying," Jackie began again, "when none of us shows up for school tomorrow, and Crazy Serena doesn't show up either, the Proper Authorities will know something's wrong."

"No, they won't," Rebecca said. "Frank Freud will be relieved to have us all gone for an entire day."

"And the school will just call in another substitute teacher for Will and Mandy," the McG said, not even commenting on the fact that we'd just referred to our principal as Frank. "Apparently, anyone can be replaced."

"Oh," Durinda said glumly.

"Say!" Annie turned to Durinda. "When Crazy Serena comes back, why don't you do that thing you do with the triple tap and the sharply pointed finger? You could freeze her right where she stands!"

"What's Annie talking about?" the McG said. "The poor girl must be delirious." She put her palm to Annie's forehead. "That's odd. You don't feel feverish."

Then, ignoring the McG's obvious confusion and because we were so bored that we needed something to do, five voices urged Durinda, "Freeze me! Freeze me!"

The only Eight's voice not urging Durinda to freeze her was Zinnia's, because, as we all knew, Zinnia was the only one of us that couldn't be frozen.

"Come on," Annie urged Durinda, who was for some reason reluctant. "It's been a long time since you've frozen anybody. You should practice up a little bit first; you know, so you'll be ready when the big moment arrives."

"Very well," Durinda at last agreed.

Durinda tapped her hand against her leg three times rapidly, then sharp-pointed at Rebecca.

We couldn't blame her for wanting to freeze Rebecca first. Rebecca could be annoying.

But nothing happened.

Rebecca remained unfrozen.

Durinda stared at the tip of her own finger as though it had somehow betrayed her.

"Must be rusty," she said with a nervous laugh and a shrug.

Then Durinda tapped her leg three times rapidly and sharp-pointed her finger at Petal, who was the second-most annoying among us.

Again, nothing.

"This is so odd!" Durinda cried.

She tried freezing Marcia.

She tried freezing Jackie.

She tried freezing Annie.

Nothing, nothing, and nothing.

In her desperation, she even tried to freeze Zinnia.

She was about to try freezing the McG when Annie reached out a hand to stop her.

"I don't think it's going to work," Annie said gently. "It's no use."

"You mean my power's all gone?" Durinda said, horrified.

"No," Annie said. "I just think that whichever Eight's month it is to get her power and gift has to figure out how to get us out of whatever jam we're in."

"So my power is temporarily on hold?" Durinda said.

"Yes," Annie said. "I think so."

"But what about you?" Durinda persisted. "You've still got your power. You're still smart."

"Yes," Annie said. "But I was already smart before all this started."

"Would someone please tell me," the McG said, "just what is going on."

But no one did, partly because we didn't know where to begin—our story was getting so involved, sometimes *we* didn't believe everything that was happening to us!—and mostly because we heard the sound of a series of locks clicking open.

Crazy Serena was back.

Behind her floated a sheet of paper.

Georgia!

Quickly, Annie circled behind Crazy Serena, snatched the floating sheet of paper out of the air, and hid it behind her back before Crazy Serena could see it.

"You must all be very tired by now," Crazy Serena said, using her sweet voice again. She was like Bad Cop and Good Cop all rolled into one person. "You must be hungry—thirsty, too. So I'll ask you again. And then, once you've given me the answers I want, we can all have that pizza I promised you earlier. *Tell me what I want to know!*"

For the first time, we realized that every time she said the word *pizza,* she said just the singular word *pizza,* not *pizzas.* Did she really think she could feed eight growing girls with just one pie? What a stingy person.

We stared back at her, silent and stony-faced. If we'd been made out of wood, we would have looked like totem poles.

"Still not talking?" Crazy Serena said, heading back to the door. "Well, let's see how good you are at keeping silent when morning comes and you haven't eaten anything since lunchtime the day before!"

Again, she was gone.

We waited a moment, then:

"Georgia," Annie whispered, "are you still here?"

We had no way of knowing if Georgia had remained with us or if she'd followed Crazy Serena back out of the room.

And then—*poof!*—Georgia was back with us.

The McG blinked. Then she put her fingers under her glasses and rubbed her eyes.

"I didn't just see that," the McG said. "A moment ago there was no Georgia and now—*poof!*—Georgia."

But there was no time for explanations.

"Just look at this," Georgia said hurriedly, grabbing the sheet of paper Annie had been holding, the better to show us what she was talking about.

"But this just looks like a normal letter," Annie said after reading it, "that hasn't been sent yet."

"But look at the signature!" Georgia said. "It says right there *Serena Smith*. Harkness isn't her last name! I found her desk and went through it. All her stationery, everything, says *Serena Smith*. Even her towels are monogrammed *SS*!"

"Am I the only one who doesn't understand why this matters?" Durinda asked.

"So Crazy Serena has a different name," Rebecca said. "So big deal."

"Smith, Smith," Marcia said. "Now, why does that name sound so familiar . . . ?"

"Because it's the same last name as *Mommy!*" Georgia said.

"It is?" Petal said.

"But I thought Mommy's last name was Huit," Zinnia said.

"It is now," Jackie said. "But before she married Daddy, her last name was Smith."

Eight minds thought about how there had been something familiar about Serena Harkness from the start. Eight minds thought about how we'd found Serena Harkness so beautiful. And now we sort of knew why.

"You don't mean," Annie said in dawning horror, "that Crazy Serena could be . . . *a relative?*"

"That's exactly what I mean!" Georgia said.

"How could we not have known about her before?" Durinda asked.

"Well," Jackie said, "Mommy and Daddy have always been very mysterious."

We had just learned something: Some relatives are teachers. Some teachers are relatives. Not all are good.

"Does this mean we have to invite her for Thanksgiving dinner?" Petal asked.

"Of course not!" Georgia said. "She's crazy as a loon! And she's evil."

That was true too and was something else we had learned:

Sometimes evil doesn't look evil or ugly. Sometimes it looks good or, worse, beautiful.

"But how could we have been so wrong about someone?" Durinda asked. It was something we all wanted to know. All of us, with the exception of Georgia, had been wrong about Crazy Serena. Well, Mandy hadn't been wrong either.

Georgia shrugged. "We were all blinded by her beauty. Even me at first."

And that was something else we had learned:

It didn't matter what people looked like; evil people were not necessarily ugly, like the Wicket. Anyone could be bad. Anyone could be good. Looks were deceiving.

"How did you know she wasn't what she seemed?" Marcia asked Georgia.

"And don't say it was just what you overheard when she was on the cell phone in the gym," Rebecca warned Georgia. "There *has* to be more to it than that!"

"We don't have time for this right now," Georgia said. "We can talk philosophy all you want once we're safely out of here. At the moment, what we need is a plan to get us all out . . . alive."

"And I suppose *you* have a plan?" Rebecca said.

"As a matter of fact, I do," Georgia said calmly. "I'll disappear again, and then you all pound on the door like crazy. Make as loud a racket as you can. When Crazy Serena comes, tell her you're ready to talk, that you'll tell her *everything,* but that there's not enough air in this room. Tell her you want to talk to her in that front room we first saw. I'll take care of the rest."

We all stared at Georgia, stunned.

Who knew she could be so commanding?

"Do it *now,*" Georgia commanded.

Then Georgia twitched her nose twice and made herself invisible again.

The McG blinked twice, but said nothing.

What else could we do?

We pounded on the door, screaming at the same time.

"That's useless," the McG told us. "I've tried that before, and trust me on this: in this house, no one can hear you scream."

But we guessed that Crazy Serena *could* hear us, because the door swung open, nearly knocking us off our feet.

We could only hope that there was more to Georgia's plan than she'd said.

CHAPTER TEN

"We'll tell you everything," Annie said.

"But first Petal needs to go to the bathroom," Durinda said.

"And Durinda needs a drink of water," Jackie said.

"Jackie could do with a cookie," Marcia said. "She's looking rather pale."

"It's very cold in this room," Rebecca said. "Didn't you pay your heating bill this month?"

"It is very hot in here," Petal said, fanning herself and wholly missing the point. Still, we loved her.

"I need to go to the bathroom too," Zinnia said, adding, "to do number two."

"So you see," Annie said, "we'll gladly tell you everything you want to know, but we'd like to do it in that nice front room and only after you've met our reasonable demands."

"I think it all does sound very reasonable," the McG said, getting into the spirit of things.

"You know," Crazy Serena said sweetly, "it *does* sound very reasonable." Then she held the door open for us. "Just so you know, though, there's no point in trying to make a run for the front door. I have the only set of keys."

Then she pointed at Petal and Zinnia. "You and you, go use the bathroom."

She pointed at Durinda and Jackie. "You and you, to the kitchen for your water and cookie."

She pointed at Rebecca. "You, take a blanket from the closet and wrap it around yourself."

She pointed to Petal. "You, take off your uniform."

"But I can't do that!" Petal tried to cover her clothed body with her hands. "Then I'd be naked!"

"Fine," Crazy Serena said, "so sweat to death. What do I care?"

She pointed at Annie and Marcia. "You and you . . . I don't remember you asking for anything." She clapped her hands. "Okay, everybody, hustle! Hustle! You need to do everything you have to and then meet me in the front room in forty-five seconds!"

Gee, she didn't expect much, did she?

And yet somehow we managed to pull it off.

We all gathered back in the front room. "Fine," Crazy Serena said, her arms crossed, her foot tapping. "I've met your demands. Now *talk*."

Crazy Serena never saw Georgia coming.

It was the wooden spoon that entered the room first, floating along, suspended in the air as though by . . .

"Magic!" Crazy Serena said, awed. "I didn't know you could do magic! Did Lucy teach you that?" she asked, saying our mother's name.

Crazy Serena wasn't as delighted when the floating spoon struck her on the shoulder.

"Hey!" she cried out, wincing.

A few moments passed, and then a frying pan entered the room and struck Crazy Serena on the rump.

Our parents had always taught us that it was wrong to be violent for the fun of it. But they'd also said that if a person is fighting for her life, almost anything goes.

And on that night, we felt as though we were fighting for our lives.

"Ouch!" after "Ouch!" after "Ouch!" informed us that Invisible Georgia was performing her pinching trick on Crazy

Serena, who kept twisting around, trying both to escape and to locate her unseen attacker.

And suddenly Georgia was *everywhere,* popping in and out of sight, making herself appear and then disappear again. It took us a while to figure it out, but eventually we caught on: Georgia was *taunting* Crazy Serena!

"Georgia!" Crazy Serena cried, at last catching a glimpse of her.

"In the flesh, *baby,*" Georgia said, then double twitched her nose and vanished again.

"Georgia Huit," Crazy Serena commanded, going all Bad Cop, "I order you to come back here!"

"Try and make me," Georgia said with a laugh.

So Crazy Serena tried being Good Cop again. "Didn't anyone ever train you to respect your elders?"

"Did they?" Invisible Georgia said, as though she couldn't decide.

Then she remembered something from our younger years. We all did.

"Mommy and Daddy always said," Invisible Georgia stated, "that everyone deserves a clean slate when you first meet them, and with that clean slate comes respect."

While Invisible Georgia spoke, Crazy Serena lunged at the space where the voice seemed to be coming from. But she was too slow, and Invisible Georgia kept dancing out of reach.

"But no one gets to keep that respect automatically,"

Invisible Georgia continued, "not if they do things to"—and here she paused as though searching for the exact word Mommy had used—"*squander* it."

"*Squander* means 'waste,'" Annie explained for the benefit of Petal and anyone else who might not know, "like when a person spends money foolishly."

"Principals don't get automatic respect for life," Invisible Georgia said, "presidents don't get automatic respect for life, and pretty substitute teachers who lie through their pretty teeth about who they are and who kidnap real teachers don't get automatic respect . . . *not* if they squander it."

In that moment, we thought that Invisible Georgia was the most gloriously gorgeous person we'd ever not seen.

Then there was a huge tearing sound—Invisible Georgia had ripped the pocket off Crazy Serena's dress!—followed by the jangle of many keys.

"Give me those back!" Crazy Serena shouted as Invisible Georgia yelled, "Annie! Catch!"

As Annie raced for the door, keys in hand, we didn't need Invisible Georgia to tell us what to do next.

We fell on Crazy Serena, figuring we'd sit on her for as long as it took Annie to get someone to help us.

It didn't take Annie long to find the help we needed. She unlocked all the many locks and threw open the door, and there stood Pete.

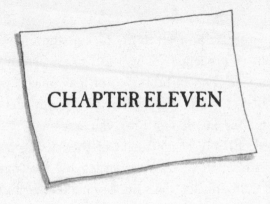

CHAPTER ELEVEN

"What are you doing here?" Annie asked, more stunned than she'd been by anything yet.

"Do you know this house is soundproof?" Pete asked. "I've been out here banging for hours." He raised his fist. His knuckles were raw.

"But how did you get here?" Annie asked. "How did you know?"

"Oh, that," Pete said. "It was that schoolmate of yours, the little redheaded one."

"Mandy?" Annie said. "Mandy *Stenko?"*

From our position on top of Crazy Serena, we could just barely see Pete's shrug.

"I dunno," he said. "I suppose that's what she's called. Anyway, just as I was leaving, she grabbed me and she told me she thought this substitute teacher of yours might be A Bad Person and that she got worried when she saw you lot getting into her car. When she told me that, I naturally jumped in my pickup and followed you here. But the teacher got you all inside before I could stop you, and then it didn't matter how much I pounded and yelled. I guess that when you're outside of this house, no one inside can hear you scream."

Just then, Pete caught sight of the McG, whom he'd met before when we'd gotten in trouble that one time.

"Oh, hullo, ducks," he said, tipping an imaginary hat as he stepped into the house. "Nice to see you again."

"You're the Eights' uncle, aren't you?" the McG said, as though wondering if wonders would ever cease.

"Er, yes," Pete said, "yes, I am, Mrs. McGillicuddy."

"Please feel free to call me Hilly," Mrs. McGillicuddy said.

Hilly? But we thought the McG's first name was Phyllis!

"It's a nickname," the McG added. "My mother used to call me that because—"

"What is this?" Crazy Serena shouted. "Old Home Week? Let me out of here!"

"Did this lady hurt you?" Pete asked us.

Eight heads nodded, plus the McG's.

"To be perfectly exact," said Georgia, who'd popped back into view just before Pete crossed the threshold and who was now sitting on Crazy Serena's back, "she hasn't really hurt us, not yet. But she wanted to."

"And she did keep me hostage here for two weeks," the McG added.

"You were right to fear me," Georgia said with satisfaction to Crazy Serena. "I am always the most trouble. You really should have kept a better eye on me." Then she laughed. "Too bad you couldn't."

Crazy Serena sneered a sneer that would have done Rebecca proud, but we weren't bothered by it.

"Leave the lady to me," Pete said.

Then he indicated that we should get off her.

We were reluctant to do so. We felt as though we were safer with all of us sitting on her back, her arms, and her legs. But we did trust Pete. So one by one, we each peeled ourselves away.

Crazy Serena scrambled to her feet, but before she could do anything, Pete grabbed her by the scruff of the

neck. Then he hustled her through the door and out onto the street.

"Get out of my town," he told her, "and stay out. And don't even *think* about coming back, because if you do, if you *ever* bother the Eights again, *I* will know it, and what I will do then, you will not like."

Then he turned her around so she was facing away from us and gave her a slight tap on the shoulder blade with one finger. It was like starting an old wind-up toy working. At first, Crazy Serena just took a stumbling step or two, but then she started moving faster until she was running down the street, racing away from us.

"*God,* you're wonderful, Mr. Pete!" Jackie cried, throwing herself at him and giving him a mighty hug.

Then we were all hugging Pete. The McG looked as though she would like to, but she hung back.

"C'mon, Eights," Pete said once we'd all hugged for long enough. "It's time to get you lot home. You've got school in the morning."

"*School?*" Rebecca said. "After what we've just been through? Don't you think we deserve a day off?"

"I'm sure your teacher won't be missing school tomorrow," Pete said, glancing at the McG, "will she?"

"Oh, I'll be there," the McG said with a firm nod of her head.

"You see?" Pete said. "Now, what kind of an uncle would I be if I let you scarper off school?"

We couldn't very well argue with that.

So we all, including the McG, climbed into the bed of Pete's pickup truck; Pete said we would drop off the McG first.

As we drove through the night, the cool wind whipping our hair, the McG had a question for us. In fact, she had more than one question.

"What happened back there?" she asked. "How did Georgia manage to disappear and then appear again? And what exactly is going on?"

After all she'd been through, we felt we owed her an explanation, but as we opened our mouths, she cut us off.

"No," she said. "Come to think of it, I don't think I want to know. In fact, I'm going to pretend none of it happened."

But she couldn't stop herself from asking one more question.

"I'm grateful, of course," she said, "to your uncle for chasing Crazy Serena out of town. But why didn't he call the police? Why didn't he have her arrested?"

It was Georgia who answered, honestly, looking the McG square in the eye. "Because then the Proper Authorities would know about us," she said. "And then they would come split us all up because we are eight little girls living at home alone."

It was hard to catch all the expressions that raced across the McG's face: shock, sadness, understanding.

At last she spoke. "I'm going to pretend I didn't hear that either," she said, "because if I had, I'd have to do something, like report it." Then: "But thank you, Eights. Thank you for finding me in that room and for keeping me company and for everything else you did. Thank you."

* * * * * * * *

We dropped off the McG, with promises to see her at school bright and early the next morning, and then went back to our own house.

Pete came inside with us.

We fed the cats, made some cocoa, and then filled Pete in on all our latest news, about how we'd tricked Crazy Serena by using Georgia's disappearing act and all the rest.

"So Georgia can really disappear now?" Pete said.

"Oh, yes," Georgia said.

"Show me," Pete said, crossing his arms.

We couldn't understand why he'd doubt us now. After all, hadn't everything we'd ever told him turned out to be true, like refrigerators who could talk and fall in love, and like Durinda being able to make everyone except Zinnia freeze? Well, we figured, maybe, like everybody else in the world, Pete just enjoyed a good show.

So Georgia twitched her nose two times and disappeared.

A moment later, Pete put his big hand to his own cheek.

"Georgia," he said, wonder in his voice, "did you just *kiss* me?"

"I did, Mr. Pete," Georgia said shyly after she'd twitched herself back into view. "It was to thank you for everything you do for us."

"This is all very *sweet,*" Rebecca said, interrupting the tender moment. "But earlier in the night, I asked Georgia how she had known that Crazy Serena really was A Bad Person after all, and I'm still waiting for my answer."

"I don't know," Georgia said, sounding puzzled. "Maybe in the same way she recognized that I was the one she needed to keep a special eye on, that I'd cause the most trouble? You were right about that, by the way. Or maybe because I'm so awful myself, I guess I just know evil when I see it."

"I don't think you're awful," Pete said to Georgia, "and I don't think you're evil."

"You don't?" Georgia asked.

"No," Pete said. "In fact, I think you're grand."

Georgia blushed.

"Now get to bed, you girls," Pete said as he rose to leave. "School in the morning!"

He paused with his hand on the doorknob.

"And you say," he asked, "that this Crazy Serena person is some sort of relative of yours?"

Eight heads nodded.

"Huh," Pete said. "The missus and I have a few like that in our families too. I suppose all families have them."

And then he was gone.

Pete had said that he and Mrs. Pete had *a few* relatives like Crazy Serena in their families? And we hadn't even known Crazy Serena *was* our relative, not until that day.

It was awesome to think that we might have other relatives we didn't know about yet, loose out there somewhere in the world.

CHAPTER TWELVE

The next day—Tuesday, March 18—when we arrived at school, it was as though none of the events of the month had happened. Crazy Serena was gone, no one was even talking about the parade anymore—it is amazing how quickly things become old news—and the McG was at her desk, looking down her long nose at us as though she smelled something bad.

In fact, we'd almost begun to doubt that any of it really had happened, but then—we swear!—the McG *winked* at us before calling the class to order. If that weren't proof enough that the universe had tilted strangely, nothing ever would be.

And there was more universe-tilting!

Right after the first class, the McG ordered us to take an early recess *outside* because it was the nicest day we'd had so far all year.

So we raced to the jungle gyms, where, hanging

upside down and such, we filled Will in on all that had happened.

"You mean Ms. Harkness really was A Bad Person?" He was stunned. "But no one guessed at first, except for Mandy."

This was true. Georgia had guessed only later; it was Mandy who knew from the start. We realized we owed her an apology. And we also owed her something else.

"Thank you, Mandy," we said, having found her playing in a corner of the playground all by herself. "Thank you for telling our friend Mr. Pete when Crazy Serena took us away in her car."

"Mr. Pete?" she said. "I thought that man was your uncle!"

Oh, dear. We hadn't meant to let *that* slip out.

So then, of course, since Mandy had done us such a good turn and proved herself to be A True Friend, we thought we should tell her, you know, *everything*.

But as we opened our mouths to speak, she stopped us, just like the McG had done the night before.

"I don't want to know," Mandy Stenko said. "Or perhaps I should say, I'm not *ready* to know." Then she paused before adding, "But I'm glad, *really* glad, that you're all okay."

And then we all played together.

Will Simms and Mandy Stenko and the eight of us.

* * * * * * * *

We arrived home that day with backpacks crammed full of homework assignments. The McG may have winked at us that morning, but she was definitely making up for lost time.

"Homework before anything else!" Annie commanded.

"No," Georgia said.

"What do you mean, no?" Annie asked.

"I need to find my gift," Georgia said.

"But it's not the right time for the return with the elixir yet," Jackie said. "That always happens at the very end of the month. I told you."

"I don't care," Georgia said. "Everything that's supposed to happen has already happened. I've discovered my power and I've even used it wisely to get us all out of trouble. *Now I want that gift!*"

Nothing could persuade Georgia differently, so we all sat back and watched as she spent the rest of the afternoon and early evening tearing the house and grounds apart.

"Did you check the mailbox?" Petal suggested.

"Yes," Georgia said.

"Have you tried summoning a pigeon to help you find it?" Zinnia said.

"No," Georgia said, "and I won't. I will have no stinking pigeons helping me this time. I want to find it myself!"

"Can I make you a cup of tea?" Durinda offered. "Perhaps that will help you focus on where it might be."

"No," Georgia said. "I still don't like tea."

Georgia was outside, digging in the neglected garden, as early evening turned into night. "Here," Annie said, bringing Georgia a coat. "At least you won't get cold."

"Take a hat too," Jackie said, slapping a hat onto Georgia's head. Then we all went back in.

"I don't think any of us has ever searched so hard for anything," Marcia observed as we all stood at the window watching Georgia continue to work her shovel, turning up great clumps of earth.

"I'm beginning to think that Georgia is as crazy as Crazy Serena," Rebecca said.

Then, at last, just as the grandfather clock in the drawing room was striking ten o'clock and we were all beginning to get drowsy, we heard a loud shout of *"Eureka!"*

A moment later, Georgia came inside, her face smudged with dirt, hair wild under her hat, and one hand clutching a golden object.

"Wherever did you find it?" Zinnia asked. "It's so pretty."

Georgia looked embarrassed. "I just found it sitting right on the ground outside the woodshed. I wish I'd thought to look there first."

"Now that you've got it," Rebecca said with a yawn, "can the rest of us go to bed? We are awfully tired."

"No," Georgia said. "First we need to go get the note from the drawing room."

So we followed her in there and watched as she removed the loose stone from the wall and took the note from the space behind.

Dear Georgia,

Six down, ten to go. And, may I add, very nicely played!

The note was unsigned.

We did still wonder who was leaving these things.

"A thought occurred to me," Georgia said, "during those many hours I spent digging outside."

"Ooh, a thought," Rebecca sneered. "Get two of those and you might have a whole idea."

Georgia ignored her. We all did.

"What is it?" Annie asked. "What was your thought?"

"It's just that it occurred to me that we might as well relax for a bit. The first note we ever got said that we *each* needed to discover our own powers and gifts in order to learn what's happened to Mommy and Daddy. We've already figured out that we each receive our power and gift, one at a time, at the rate of one sister per month. It stands to reason, then, that we won't have everything we need until *after* Zinnia's discovered her power and gift, which will be sometime in the month of August."

"I do wish I didn't have to wait that long," Zinnia said with a heavy sigh.

"So you see," Georgia said, "since we won't have everything we need before August, we might as well settle in and enjoy the ride."

"However bumpy that ride might prove to be," Jackie said. But she didn't sound as though she was complaining. She sounded as though she was excited. And who could blame her? April—her month—was next.

"At least we don't have Crazy Serena to worry about anymore," Marcia said.

"But who knows what other sort of awful person will pop up next?" Petal said.

"Whatever happens," Annie said, "we'll handle it."

"With occasional help from Pete," Jackie said.

"And Will," Durinda added.

"Maybe even Mandy," Zinnia said.

"But what are you going to do with that compact?" Rebecca asked Georgia. "You said you don't even like compacts."

"I know," Georgia said. "But maybe I could use the mirror in it to start fires by focusing the light of the sun?" She shrugged. "I'm sure it will come in handy at some point. Nearly everything always does, except when it doesn't."

"If you don't like it," Zinnia said timidly, "you could always give it to—"

"No!" Georgia said, clutching the golden compact to her chest. "I've worked hard for it, dug in the dirt for it, and it's mine, I tell you, mine, mine, mine!"

On another night, one of us might have accused Georgia of being selfish. What, after all, is the point of clutching tightly to something if a person doesn't even *like* that something?

But we couldn't criticize her, not on that night. When we were imprisoned at Crazy Serena's, Invisible Georgia could have escaped alone and left us to fend for ourselves. And yet Georgia hadn't done that. Rather, Georgia had done so much, so much to save *us.*

So, instead:

"Three cheers for Georgia!" seven voices shouted. "Hip, hip, hooray!"

Even Rebecca cheered.